Sapphire Eyes

The Club Red Series

By Aurelia Yates

ISBN: 979-8-9867542-3-9

WARNING

'This book is rated R; not appropriate for readers under 18 years of age; contains elements of violence, sexual abuse.

TABLE OF CONTENTS

1

Rose

I've had a really shitty day. First, I woke up with a headache because I'd stayed up most of the night, stressing over my parents.

They had called me to let me know they wouldn't be able to pay my tuition any longer. Their business has taken a hit, and they're having extreme cutbacks. Then, this morning, I was late to work. When I finally made it, I was laughed at, only to discover that their laughter was from my inability to realize I had left my apartment with two completely different shoes. Plus, my shirt was inside out. At lunchtime, one of my bosses demanded that I work through my lunch to finish his transcripts. I'm so relieved that it's finally five o'clock.

I'm off work, heading to Hunter's apartment to

surprise him. I told him I was planning on hanging with Liz, but she canceled at the last minute.

Hunter and I have been dating for three months. He said he knew I was the one for him the first time he saw me.

I'm about to knock on his door when it opens, and Trey—his roommate, walks out. He's too distracted with his phone to notice I'm standing at the doorframe. I don't even bother to speak. Trey has been an ass from day one.

Before the door shuts, I stretch out my hand to stop it. Entering the apartment, I closed the front door. Behind me, I hear someone moaning. I smile, thinking Hunter must be watching porn.

Maybe it's time we take this relationship to another level.

We haven't had sex yet. I want to wait till I feel the time is right.

As I approach Hunter's bedroom door, I see it's ajar. Slowly, I push it open. I don't believe the scene that my eyes are taking in. This day keeps getting shittier.

Hunter is standing behind a girl, slapping her ass, yelling, "Who's your daddy?"

They keep going at it, not even aware of my presence.

Tears well up in my eyes.

I scream out, "You jerk!"

Hunter freezes. His back stiffens. He doesn't even bother turning around. He keeps his cock buried in the girl's ass. I cannot make out her face because it's turned in the opposite direction of my sight.

Not waiting for him to reply, I run straight from his apartment to mine. Not caring how far the distance is between our buildings. My mind is too preoccupied with the picture of Hunter behind that girl.

When I enter my apartment, I collapse, letting the tears flow freely down my face. It's not like we spent years together, but I thought maybe, just maybe, this time, I had found my special person. I'm so humiliated to think that I was letting myself fall for him. I trusted all the sweet words that spilled out of his rotten mouth.

My cell phone rings, pulling me out of my self-pity. Raising my head to view my phone screen, I can see it's dark outside now. I must have been lying on the floor longer than I realized. Seeing the caller is my mom, I wipe the tears from my face, trying to get my composure together. I don't want to worry my parents about my minor trouble when their issues are much more significant than a breakup.

"Hey, mom." I try my best to sound cheerful.

"Sweetie, are you okay? You sound upset."

I knew she would pick up on my mood.

"I'm good. Just super busy. I have to go. Liz is on the other line. Let me call you later," I lie.

I need to get off this phone. I want a massive glass of wine to help wash the memories of a specific person away.

Once we say our good-byes, I grab a glass from the cabinet. Uncorking the wine, I pour it to the rim.

My phone rings again, but this time, when I look at the caller ID, I see it's Hunter.

If he thinks I want anything to do with him, he's deranged.

Allowing the call to go to voice mail, I take a huge gulp of wine. I definitely need it after the day I have had.

My cell pings, letting me know it's a text.

Rose, pick up. I know you see me calling you. We need to talk.

My blood boils at seeing he wants to talk.

Talk about what? How his dick fell into some girl's ass. Nope. He doesn't get another chance. Once a cheater, always a cheater.

I have other things to worry about right now, like, how I will pay for my law school. My parents can no longer pay for both of their daughter's tuition. Since I already have most of my education, they decided to pay for my sisters because Lilly just finished high school with a partial college scholarship. Which means they will have to pay for the remainder of her tuition.

I have close to a year left in school and desperately want to finish. I have wanted to pursue a career in law for as long as I can remember. Interning as a legal secretary at Ross and Archer in New York, which happens to be the largest law firm in Manhattan, will help start me in the right direction for my career. However, being an intern doesn't pay very well. Thankfully, when they had money, Mom and Dad purchased an apartment for me.

***

I'm sitting at my desk at Ross and Archer when Liz comes to get me for lunch.

"Taco Tuesday," Liz says while she shakes her hips.

"Yes!" I spring from my chair.

I love our Taco Tuesdays.

I grab my purse while we march out the door.

Less than five ten minutes we are seated at Taco Mom's and the waitress takes our order. Once she leaves, I tell Liz about how I caught Hunter's dick in someone's ass.

"I always thought he was a cunt," she remarks.

Shrugging my shoulders, I say, "I believed everything he said about us being together. He tried to call and text me all last night."

"Did you speak to him?" she questions.

I shake my head. "No, I don't want to. I'm afraid he might try to sell me some bullshit. I'm not buying it. I know his dick didn't fall into that girl. I don't want to hear excuses."

Liz looks over to a table then let's out a small gasp. Her head jerks around to look out the window while she shields her face with her hand. I turn to look at what she was gasping at. It's a tall man with a blue suit on. His broad shoulders seem to be stretching the material of the coat. The little amount of premature salt in his bread gives him a very fuckable vibe.

"Liz, who is that?"

She doesn't reply. Liz looks shocked and *I don't want to be here,* is written on her face.

"It's no one," she replies.

If that's no one, I would hate to see how she reacted to it being someone. I draw closer to her in hopes that no one hears me.

"If he's no one, why are you hiding?"

She stares at me. I imagine she's trying to decide how much information she wants to tell me.

"Hey, why don't we go to Club Z on Friday night? I'll invite Vinnie," she says to the window.

I can tell she is avoiding the subject.

"Are you not going to tell me why you are hiding behind your hand?"

I look at the table where the man sits with two other men. They're all huge! His friends have their backs to us, but then Mr. Sex On Legs looks up, and our eyes meet only for a brief moment before he moves them to soak Liz in. I wonder if he's an ex-boyfriend. He gets out of his chair and takes wide steps in our direction.

"Oh shit, Liz, he's coming over here."

She curses, "Shit, do I have time to leave?"

I whisper, "Nope, too late."

I look up at him and notice how large the man that stands at the end of our table is. His eyes are set on Liz, with heat in them. I would give anything for a man that gorgeous to have eyes for me like that. I swear, I think the fire department needs to be called because the lustful look he is giving her could cause panties to ignite. Sensing Liz is going to refrain from speaking, I offer to speak first.

"Hello," I look at him like maybe he's lost. "Can I help you?"

He gives me a lopsided smile, showing some of the prettiest white teeth.

"I'm wondering if your friend … Liz, plans on

avoiding me or if she is going to speak," he says in a deep voice with a hint of an accent.

Liz finally turns her head slowly in the direction of the stranger. "Hi, Mark," she squeaks out.

This time, he gives a smile displaying all his perfect teeth.

"I wasn't trying to avoid you. My mind was preoccupied," she lies.

He stands at the end of the table, eyeing Liz.

"How are you? I haven't seen you in some time, but I have been on," he stops, then looks over to me—, "business."

"That's great! Oh, look, our food is here."

Liz fakes a smile at Mark. He moves out of the waitress's way.

Then, she cuts him off, "Well, it was good to see you. Have a nice day." She grabs her fork, turning her full attention to her plate.

I give him a smile and a small wave. Wow, Liz blew him off big time. Wonder what he did to her. I watch him as he goes back to his seat.

Turning my focus on Liz, I watch as she devours her food.

"Rose, you didn't answer my question."

I look at her with confusion. "What question?" I ask.

"Do you want to go out on Friday night?" she repeats.

I exhale. I haven't been out since I started dating Hunter. He didn't want me to go to clubs unless he was with me. I'm not sure if I feel up to it.

"I don't know," I tell my plate of tacos.

"Rose, look at me."

I can feel the tears in the backs of my eyes, fighting to come out. Crap, I'm afraid they will make their way down my cheeks if I look at her.

"Rose, please look at me," Liz begs.

I raise my head and make eye contact with her, hoping my tears will remain in the back of my eyes.

"He wasn't good for you," she gives me a small smile.

"It's not just him. I need to get a second job. My parents are not able to fund my tuition any longer." I exhale, feeling a weight off my shoulders. It feels good to tell someone.

She looks at me, blinking. I know it was a load to dump on her.

"Shit, I didn't mean to drop my troubles on you. It's my problem don't worry about it. I will find another job and then everything should be better."

Liz looks around us as if the FBI might be staking us out. When she feels it's safe for her to speak, she leans over the table, holding her finger up, motioning for me to come closer.

"I might be able to help you, but you cannot tell a single person. What I'm about to tell you I do NOT want my business to get out. It could hurt my chances of becoming a lawyer," Liz whispers.

I nod. *What could it be? Is Liz a drug lord?* Now, I'm afraid to know.

She continues, "That guy, Mark ..."

I nod, afraid to speak.

"He knows me from my part-time job." She pauses, then looks around again. "I work at a high-class brothel."

She pauses again, looking at me, as if waiting for a reaction.

"Do you understand what I'm saying?" she asks.

I frown. "You mean, you're a hooker?"

"I don't like that word. A high-class call girl is better. Hooker sounds … well it sounds nasty," she says with her nose scrunched up.

"Okay … so you're a call girl, and that guy was your customer?" I ask, trying to make sure I'm processing the information correctly.

Now, it's her turn to nod.

"No. Are you serious?" I scream out.

"Keep your voice down," Liz hisses. "He was a customer till I found out who he is."

I blink in surprise. She's serious. "Liz, no disrespect, but I don't want that type of work. It's not for me."

She smiles. "Rose, I know that. I have seen the way you shy away from guys, the ones who are out for one thing. I bet you didn't have sex with Hunter. Did you?"

I shake my head. "I was thinking about it. I guess a part of me knew he was a cheater. Looking back on it now, I'm glad I didn't. I wonder if he was trying to get into my panties."

"When the time is right, you will know and won't

second-guess yourself … until then, enjoy being single. You know, the club has so many rich, good-looking men. My boss has a position as a waitress. If you want, I can put in a good word for you."

I need the money, but working at a place that sells sex? I'm not so sure.

Sensing my hesitation, Liz gives me a little encouragement.

"Just come check it out. You will make ten times more working as a waitress at Club Red than anywhere else. How do you think I can afford everything I do and pay for school? I'm not saying be a call girl. Just come and have a peek for yourself."

2

Rose

After giving my word, and the fact that my savings are almost depleted, I told Liz I would at least explore the idea of working for a place such as Club Red.

I'm on my way to meet Liz and check out the atmosphere at Club Red when Hunter calls my phone—again. He has been calling non-stop.

I sigh. "Hello?"

"Rose, can we meet to talk, please?" Hunter begs.

"Hunter, there's nothing to talk about. I don't want to see you anymore."

"I'm sorry. I made a mistake. I miss you, Rose. Please give me another chance," he begs.

No way in hell I'm going back to him. I want someone fully committed to me. Someone who only has eyes for me. I don't want a man who wants to bury his dick into someone's ass that's not mine. Scratch that I don't want that, period.

"No, I—" he cuts me off.

"Rose, meet me. That's all I ask."

I exhale. "Fine, I will, but I have to go."

"Rose, you're still the one for me," Hunter breathes into the phone.

I roll my eyes at his comment. "Bye, Hunter." Without waiting for him to say good-bye, I hang up.

When I arrive at the address Liz gave me, I'm a little taken aback. It's at the far end of the city. The building appears to look like an abandoned factory with blacked-out windows. Trying to gather my nerves, I walk up to the door. It's large, and it looks to be made out of steel. I try to turn the handle, but it's locked. I knock twice, waiting for someone to answer the door. I take in the surroundings. If it wasn't for the flashy cars in the front of the building, it would appear to be an abandoned building.

When the door swings open, a very large man with blond hair, and the most hypnotizing blue eyes stands in the doorway. I take a step back. To say he intimidates me is an understatement.

He's wearing a cobalt-blue dress shirt, rolled up on his forearms. The color makes his sapphire eyes shine bright. I take in his body. The rippling muscles on his arms, the strong jawline he possesses, and the tattoos that crawl up under the sleeves of his shirt and peek out of his collar. The man screams badass.

He scans me from the toe of my shoes to the top of my head, and when his eyes come back to meet mine, he gives me a wicked grin. He has to be the most breathtaking man. I have had the pleasure of sharing the same space with.

I'm barely able to get the words out. "I'm here to see Liz Black."

His tongue darts out, licking his lips, and then his teeth slowly pull in his bottom lip. I try my best not to seem effected by his good looks, but it appears the cocky bastard notices how much he has affected me. My attention is tuned in to how long and thick his tongue is. Holy Mother Teresa, my mind is in overdrive as to what he could do with that weapon.

"Blaze," he says with a silky voice.

"Blaze?" I say with a wrinkle between my brows.

The god says, "My name is Blaze."

He steps aside for me to enter. Once he closes the door, he walks around me to lead me down a dark hallway. I cannot help but take in the view of his backside. His muscular shoulders seem too big for his shirt. Not to mention, he has a perfect, fit ass.

My attention focuses back on where I am when he opens a door. I walk through the door, mesmerized by how beautiful the large area is. The appearance of the building from the outside gives no credit to how the inside looks. It's as if I stepped into a completely different structure. The plush velvet material hangs down to give the illusion of windows with large crystal chandeliers hanging over the sitting areas. The elegant mahogany wood accents surround the bar and stage. The whole place screams luxury.

I'm blindsided when Liz crashes into me.

"You made it!" she exclaims as she hugs me like it's the first time we have seen each other in years.

Blaze is now sitting at the end of the bar with his blazing blue eyes zeroed in on me. I look back to Liz, wanting to focus on her, but the man who led me in keeps drawing my attention. Especially since I can feel his eyes roaming my body.

Keep yourself in check Rose. I tell myself.

"It's stunning," I tell her.

Liz claps her hands together. "I want you to meet my boss, Candy."

A lady who looks to be in her mid-thirties comes up standing beside Liz. She takes a step back, giving me a once-over. I smile, trying my best to keep my nerves under control.

"Hi. Welcome to Club Red," she greets me. "I think you will fit in nicely. I can show you a room if you'd like and go over all the details about what to expect from your clients."

I open my mouth to tell her I'm here for the waitress position, but I get cut off when a rough voice booms from behind me, making me jump.

"No, she won't be in a room. Only on the floor, waiting tables, nothing more."

Shivers run up my spine at the sound of the deep voice coming from my back. I turn, narrowing my eyes, it's Blaze. He's standing behind me with a hair distance between us. I can feel his breath on my face. Trying to keep my strength I compose myself.

"I can speak for myself, thank you," I tell the

arrogant asshole.

I don't want to be a call girl, but I won't let a man, especially someone I don't know, tell me what I can and cannot do. We stand only centimeters apart with an intense emotion between us. Staring into his sapphire eyes, I can't help but feel a little arousal. The man is quite a hunk.

Hunter never made my body react this way. Even when he tried to feel me up. Damn this man with his good looks and sexy accent.

Turning to Candy, I say, "I would very much like to see the rooms and the rest of the club."

She gives me a grin, then winks at me. "This way."

She goes to walk up a staircase. I follow suit, and I can still feel his eyes on me. When I glance in the direction where he stood, he's still standing in the same spot, eyeing me. He's saying something, I imagine, in his native tongue. I have no doubt he's pissed. The way his hands are clenching at his sides is a dead giveaway.

Once we are out of Blaze's hearing range, I tell Candy that I'm only interested in the waitress position, but that I am grateful for the other opportunities she offered. She understands. Candy says not everyone is cut out to be a call girl. However, if I ever change my mind, all I have to do is let her know, and she would move me up. I'm so glad she is cool about me not wanting to be a call girl. Honestly, I never will be interested in that sort of work. I don't want to tell Candy or Liz that bit of information.

Candy gives me the option to start working tonight, but I decline. I have studying to do tonight. Plus, I need to do laundry. I have been a little bit lazy lately.

After arriving home and finishing my class work, I sit on the couch, catching up on my favorite television series, while I eat my weight through French fries. My cell pings with an incoming text, but I don't recognize the sender.

Tomorrow, be at the club at five sharp.
I text back.
Will do, Candy. Thank you again for the job.
A text immediately bounces back,
Blaze.

My heartbeat picks up when I know it's Blaze. I'm so nervous as, I stare at the phone. Another text comes in from a different unknown number.

You're going to pay for what you did.
This has to be a mistake. I dismiss the text.

I decide to call my sister to check in on her. She informs me she wants to come to visit soon. I haven't seen Lilly since after she graduated high school. I feel guilty because I didn't get to make her graduation. I was afraid to take time off from my internship. Lucky for me, my family understood. Instead of Lilly going on her senior week with her friends, she came to spend a week with me. A part of me thinks that she didn't get to go with her friends to travel for two weeks due to our parents' lack of funds. Mom had mentioned they were starting to lose customers then.

"Lilly, what about school?" I question her, knowing she is in the middle of a semester.

"Just for a few days. I want to see you. Miss you."

I know Lilly better than she knows herself. Her wanting to visit me only gives me a vibe that something is wrong.

"Sounds great, but I'm starting a new job, so give me a heads-up when you plan to come. I'll have to ask for time off."

She replies, "Will do. I will see you in two weeks!"

***

The following day, when I wake up, I feel a smile spread across my face. The first genuine smile in days. Still having the same smile plastered on my face when I arrive at work, I stop at Liz's desk. Excitement fills me as I tell her about Lilly's visit.

"Are you starting tonight?" Liz whispers to me.

"I am. I hope I don't spill drinks everywhere or on someone," I tell her, whispering back.

Liz moves her eyes in the direction of the open office doors. It's as if we can sense when the office snitch is coming. We automatically stop speaking till Stevie sits at her desk.

"No, you won't. You'll be fine. Just make sure to smile and bounce your cleavage. That always draws in more money."

I laugh.

"Have you heard from Hunter?"

"Yes, he wants to meet to talk." I sigh.

The last thing I want to discuss is Hunter. I have no idea what to say to him. At night, when I lie down, I still have the picture of him fucking that chick.

"I think you should tell him, to fuck off."

"I should but I'm trying to avoid speaking to him altogether. I need to get back to work. I'll see you during lunch." I wave bye as I head in the direction of my desk.

Later in the evening, I am about to leave my desk at Ross and Archer when Mr. Wallace, one of the lawyers I work for, walks out of his office.

"Rose, I know you are about to head off, but I need this letter typed up. It needs to be served to a witness tonight."

Double shit I have an hour before I begin my first shift at Club Red. I have to go home to change.

"Yes, sir." Taking the paper from him, I start to type it up.

Mr. Wallace is an extremely good-looking man in his mid-thirties, single, and considering the number of clients he brings in, he has to be making good money.

He works entirely too much. The word is that his penis is enormous, and he's a beast in bed! I don't know how that information was leaked, but it must hold some truth because most of the women in the office have put more effort into letting him know they are available. He doesn't seem to show interest in any of them. He rarely speaks to anyone, except me, mostly small talk. When he does speak, it's usually work-related.

I think it's due to me being the only lady in the office who doesn't stare at his crotch while he speaks.

Feeling the pressure of needing to be on time for my first day at Red, when I see Liz, I run up to her.

"Liz, Mr. Wallace asked me to type this letter up for him. I still need to go home to change clothes before my shift starts. Would you please type this one up for me?"

"Of course," she says.

I'm so grateful. I hug her and then kiss her cheek.

"Give it to the carrier so it will get served tonight. Will I see you tonight?"

"Yes, my first client," She clears her throat. "Seven tonight."

Thanking her again, I leave to get dressed for my shift.

3

Rose

When I arrive at work, I'm wearing the standard uniform Candy gave me. It's a cute red midriff top with an extremely low V-neck that enhances my breasts, paired with black shorts. I top the outfit off with dressy black sandals. I look like I'm going out to enjoy myself at a club, not to work at one.

Getting out of my car, I walk to the door and knock. Only this time, it's not Blaze who opens the door. It's a younger guy, around my age. He's tall and lean, and his hair is pulled back in a man bun. He smiles. It's a wide grin on his handsome face. Well, shit, do all the men that work here have to be so good-looking?

"Hey, sweetheart. You must be Rose," he says in a seductive voice.

I smile back and nod.

"I'm Brady, security. Your safety will be my number one priority." He gives me a wink.

I raise my eyebrows at that. When someone clears their throat, I look past Brady. Blaze is standing there with an angry look plastered on his face.

"Brady, go make yourself useful," Blaze commands.

Blaze must be the boss because Brady winks again and walks off without a fuss. When my eyes make their way in Blaze's direction, I notice his eyes fill with lust as he stares at my breasts. When his eyes finally rise to mine, I can feel the heat intensify in my stomach. Just from a single look, he causes my body to react.

"Rose."

I peel my eyes away from Blaze to the direction of a voice calling me. It's Candy. She motions me to come to her.

After Candy settles me in, I start training with Angel. She's a waitress. She's cute, sweet, and she has an excellent knack for flirting with men to make more significant tips. I need to keep in mind some of those tricks she uses when I'm on my own.

Liz was right about making more money here. I swear we have only waited on a handful of customers, but I have made more tonight than I do at Ross and Archer in a week. The men are respectful—for the most part.

One guy made the comment that he would like to take us both back to a room and show us his anaconda. I'm guessing it looks more like a tapeworm than an anaconda. Lucky for us, Brady walked by just as the dipshit made his remark. Mr. Anaconda took one look at Brady and made the wise choice to keep his rude comments to himself.

After several hours, when things finally slowed down, Angel release me on my own. She thought I was doing a great job. Lucky for me, her section is next to mine in case I need her.

I'm enjoying myself as I work my tables, ensuring my customers are taken care of. When I'm taking a new customer's order, I feel as if someone is watching me. It doesn't require me to look. I know who it is because he's been sitting on the same barstool for the majority of the night, watching me. *Does he not have anything else to do?*

It's finally my break time. Gathering my order, I head to my only table with customers. When they're settled with their drinks in front of them, I start to leave the floor, heading out on my break. Before I'm able to, Felix,—the bartender yells over the music.

"Rose, I'm swamped here. Can you be a doll and go to the storage room and grab two tequila bottles for me?"

I don't want to be a bitch, but I was looking forward to going on break.

"Yeah, no problem," I yell back to Felix.

When Candy came to me earlier, she gave me another tour of the place. She said from time to time, the bar would ask the waitresses for help.

I'm in the storage room, looking for the bottles of tequila, when I hear a clicking noise. I jump up on a chair, hearing laughter coming from behind me—Brady. He's standing by the doorway, clutching his stomach and bending over.

"You should have seen the look on your face." He continues to laugh.

I feel my face blush from embarrassment.

With my hand on my chest, I say breathlessly, "Shit, you scared me. I thought it was a mouse."

When the door opens again, Blaze is standing in the doorway. His eyes are intense, filled with a fire in them. However, his eyes are not set on me, they're on Brady.

"Brady, didn't I tell you to make yourself useful? Go keep an eye on the girls up front. Rose doesn't require your attention," Blaze snarls.

I snap back at Blaze for being such an ass, "He's not bothering me. Thank you for your concern, but you can leave." I turn my head so that his gorgeous features don't distract me.

I spot the liquor Felix was asking for. *Thank goodness. I'm so ready to get out of here.*

"Hold this, please." I pass a bottle of liquor to Brady as I grab the second bottle. "I need to take these to Felix."

Brady smiles at me, and he's just so cute that I can't help but smile back.

I'm too into Brady's smile when, suddenly, the bottle of alcohol is jerked out of my hand, slamming into Brady's chest.

"Take these to Felix, and then get your arse back to looking after the girls," Blaze demands.

I feel the tension in the air as Brady and Blaze bore holes into each other's eyes. Trying to cut the friction in the air. I offer to take the liquor.

"I can take th—."

Blaze cuts me off, "Brady will do it."

Watching Brady leave, I start to move to the door, but Blaze wraps his large hand around my wrist, holding me back. He looks down at me. His height towers over me. His eyes are a darker shade of their perfect sapphire color. My heartbeat picks up as heat floods my core.

Damn hormones. Just being this close to him is making my body react in ways it shouldn't.

I try to pull my arm away, but when I do, his free hand wraps around my throat. I should be afraid. Afraid of him and the burning flames in his eyes. Somehow, I'm more afraid of getting lost in these feelings for him. Allowing myself to indulge in Blazes' lips would not be wise. With our eyes locked on each other, he leans down as he guides his hand up my throat to cup my cheek. His lips brush against mine. I can feel my eyes fluttering. Dear God, the pulse between my thighs is throbbing. I bite the inside of my cheek before I let out a moan. The heat in my sex escalates as he presses his erection into me.

Keep calm, Rose, I tell myself.

When he speaks, his voice is husky. "Mo Rós darling." *Translation: My darling Rose.*

I don't understand what he just said, but I allow my eyes to close for a moment to soak in his closeness.

Get it together Rose.

I need to get out of here before I lose all of my

good-girl senses. This man is sexy and infuriating, and I want him. He's not the kind of man I need to have in my life. I need a man who is caring and devoted. I don't think Blaze is that man. Just like Hunter, I'm sure his silky tongue has mastered the art of using words to get his way.

Finally getting the strength, I push him from me. I bolt out of the storage room without even bothering to look back. If I look back, I'm afraid my willpower to keep a distance from him will crumble. My body wants his powerful arms to hold me tight as he guides his tongue through my lips to devour me while my heart tells me he's no good and to run.

The rest of the night goes uneventfully, thank goodness. I finish with my last customer and clean the last booth in my section; when I notice Liz walking down the stairs. She looks really tired. Hopefully, she can get some rest tonight since we don't have to go to work or class tomorrow.

"Liz," I call out to her before she's able to get to the door.

She's barely able to keep her eyes open. I walk over to her.

"Hey, you okay?"

"Yeah, just tired," she replies.

"Do you want to go to your favorite coffee shop for brunch tomorrow?"

That seems to perk her up. A smile spreads across her neutral face.

"Yes. Does ten o'clock sound okay?" She remarks enthusiastically.

"Do you have a way home tonight?"

"Yes."

"I will see you tomorrow." I hug Liz.

When she leaves, I hurry to gather my things from my locker. I want to avoid seeing Blaze before I leave. The scene in the storage room has been replaying in my mind all night. If I'm being honest with myself, I could have given in so easily because,—let's face it,—those blue eyes with that hard body could melt any girl's panties right off.

***

The next morning, I'm sitting at our usual table, waiting for Liz, when the door rings, letting everyone know that someone has entered the shop. I look up, expecting Liz, but to my surprise, it's Blaze.

What the hell is he doing here?

I do my best to keep my head down, only to fail when I feel him standing at my side.

I don't recall ever seeing him in here before.

Liz and I always come to this shop for some type of beverage or a snack. Not bothering to speak, the man just makes himself comfortable in the seat across from me. I look up to see a smirk on his face.

"Are you playing hard to get?" he says with amusement dancing in his eyes.

Damn his good looks.

"I … I was looking at the menu," I lie to some degree. I do have the menu in my hand.

He laughs.

It has to be the sexiest laugh I have ever heard.

"That seat is saved for someone."

The expression on his face goes from friendly to him flexing his jaw with cold eyes observing my face.

"Who?" he says as he grinds his teeth.

"It's none of your business. Now, leave," I whisper over the table to him.

He retorts, "No." He glares at me with narrowed eyes. "Not until you tell me whom you're meeting."

I'm fuming over the audacity of his demands of wanting to find out about my business. I almost feel like stomping my feet like a toddler but choose not to for fear of causing a scene.

"Fine, I'm meeting Liz. Now you can leave."

He stands but leans over the edge of the table. He's close. So close that I can see the stubble that is barely appearing on his beautiful face.

"*Mo Rós darling,* I plan on owning all of you. Don't let another man touch what is mine. It will only get him killed. I don't plan on sharing you."

My jaw drops at his words.

He puts his forefinger under my chin to close it.

"These lips …." In a smooth motion, he glides his thumb over my bottom lip. "These lips were made to be wrapped around my cock."

Oh God. Those words have me almost sliding out of my seat. Still stunned by his words, I sit in my chair, watching him as he turns around and walks out the door. Liz walks into the shop as he exits. Blaze gives her a chin up to acknowledge her presence.

Liz looks to be stupefied by seeing Blaze.

That makes two of us.

She doesn't even wait till she is seated to question me.

"What the hell, Rose? Why is Blaze here? Don't tell me you slept with him."

I exhale, sinking into my chair more. "No, I am not sleeping with him. He just showed up. I've never seen him here before." I wonder how much she knows about Blaze.

"Well … good. Have you ordered anything?"

That was short. Has she slept with him? I feel my cheeks heat up. Just thinking of Liz with Blaze makes me feel … could it be jealousy? No, that can't be it. I have never been jealous of any man. I want more information; I need more information.

"Liz, tell me, what do you know about Blaze?" I'm hoping she will give the dish on him, but I don't want to sound desperate.

Liz looks up at me from her menu. "He's a playboy. He has been with several of the girls at the club. He's only interested in getting what he wants, and then he moves on. Rumor has it, there have been several catfights over him. Apparently, he must have one mighty dick."

Well, if it's as impressive as I felt last night, I have a feeling it is a mighty dick. The way he pressed up against me in the storage room. I could feel how hard and thick it was.

Still wanting to know if she has been with him, I try to poke for more information.

"Have you been with him?" I say with my best non-interested voice.

"No."

Whew, that takes a load off my mind. I love Liz, but I don't want someone that she has had. I might not measure up to her talents. I have only been with one man—or I should say, boy. Shortly after turning eighteen in the twelfth grade, I lost my virginity to the high school quarterback at a party. When he told his buddies, I was mortified. I'd listened to all his sweet words, sucked in like a fool. I won't let that happen again. No matter how hot someone is.

4

Rose

A week later, I'm sitting on the couch in my apartment, enjoying me time, painting my toenails, and trying to catch up on my favorite television series. I pick up the nail polish and start to close the bottle when someone knocks on my door.

Looking out the peep hole, I see it's Lilly. I open the door in a rush, "Lilly!" I scream.

I embrace her in a bear hug. She pats me on my lower back in a silent signal to let her go.

"Lilly, what the hell? You should have called me. I didn't think you were coming this soon."

She pushes me into the apartment and slams the door shut. The look of horror sits on her face.

"Lilly, what the hell is wrong?" I take her by the

shoulders, forcing her to look at me.

Her breaths are hard, like she has ran up all the flights of steps to get into the apartment.

Lilly's face is pale when I move my hands to hers. They're clammy. I pull her to the couch and tell her to sit.

"Lilly, are you okay?" I question her again.

Taking a few short breaths to control herself, she breathes out, "I think someone was following me."

"What makes you think that?" I ask.

"I just had a bad feeling, like someone was watching me the whole time since I arrived at the airport."

"Why don't you go wash up? It's been a long flight. I'm sure a little rest will help you feel better." I convince her.

After Lilly washes up, she lies down to grab a nap. That's when my mind travels to Blaze and how he warned me not to let another man touch me. Was he serious?

I need to stop thinking about him. He's not the relationship type, only the fuck-buddy type. Could I just have a fuck buddy with no feelings developing? *No, Rose. No!*

***

It's five in the evening the next day. I'm headed home to get ready to work tonight at Club Red. When I step up to the elevator, Mr. Wallace makes conservation.

"Rose, do you have plans for tonight?"

Why, yes, I'm going to wait tables at a strip club. Care to join?

"No, not really, just hanging out with my sister.

She's in town."

Which isn't a lie, just not the complete truth.

Trying to turn the conservation around, I say, "You're leaving early tonight, Mr. Wallace. Do you have plans?"

"Meeting some associates for a drink."

When we walk out of the building, we say our good-byes, heading separate ways.

I rush into my apartment, undressing from the moment I close my front door. When I go into my bedroom, I throw my clothes in a basket. Doing my best not to trip over myself. I don't want to be late.

Lilly comes into my bedroom as I dart into the bathroom, almost knocking her over.

"Sorry," I yell out as I slam the door.

"Where are you going in such a hurry?" she asks, standing outside the bathroom door.

"I have to work tonight," I yell back.

"Where are you working?"

I'm not prepared to answer that question. What do I say? Do I tell her the truth? A lie? She's my sister, yet I don't want my parents to find out. I don't want them to feel guilty about where I chose to work to get money for my classes. I finish up in the bathroom, opening the door to find Lilly still standing outside the door.

"I'm a waitress." That is all I give her.

"Where at? I would like to come and hang out."

No, I don't think so. She couldn't even get into the club because she's underage.

"You're underage, Lilly." I remind her.

"I have a fake ID!" she says with a gleam in her eyes.

"No freaking way. Give it to me," I demand.

The last freaking thing I need is for her ass to come to Red.

"Hell no!" she states. "I get into all the great clubs back at school, and I'm coming to hang out at your bar tonight."

What the fuck? "Lilly …" I exhale.

Now is the time to tell her because I know her busybody ass will show up. She's determined I know her.

"I. Do. Not want Mother and Father to find out. Promise me." I look at her, deadpan.

Confusion on her face, she says, "Okay."

Cringing, as I speak the words, "I wait tables at a strip club."

A smile spreads across her face. "Well, well, little Miss. Square has finally decided to step out of her perfect box."

"I'm not a square … just cautious." I roll my eyes. "I like to have fun, you know. I'm just the responsible type for having fun."

I kiss her on the cheek. "I have to go. Love you."

I don't bother to stop to listen to what she is saying. I run out the door.

***

It's busy tonight at the club. I haven't been able to take a break all night. I've looked around for Blaze, who is usually sitting at the end of the bar, but he's not been in sight.

"Rose, a new customer at table ten," Felix yells from across the bar. I'm so tired from the crowd tonight. I have completely zoned out. I try to shake it off, walking over to take table ten's order. When I get to the table, I look up to see Mr. Wallace with three other good-looking men.

Oh shit! The last thing I want is to have one of my bosses here.

It's too late now. He looks from his friend to me. We continue to look at each other as his friends are smiling, looking back and forth between us.

I clear my throat. "What can I get you gentlemen to drink?"

I turn my head to start with the guy to the right. He's good-looking, and he resembles Mr. Wallace, but a slightly younger version. Taking everyone's order, I turn to the last gentleman in the booth, who just happens to be my boss.

"For you sir what would you like to drink?"
He smiles.

I have to say, he looks delicious tonight. Wearing blue jeans with a sports coat.

"Rose"—he rolls the R, as if he just tasted something sinfully sweet—"nice to see you. I didn't know you worked here."

Does that mean he comes here often?

"Yes, I just started a couple of weeks ago," I remark.

"Do you work in the back as well?" he says looking me up and down.

I feel my cheeks heat up. "No, only the tables."

"Well, I'm sure you leave a lot of men disappointed, only working the tables."

My mouth drops.

"Do you want me to show his ass out?" I hear a voice behind me say.

When I turn around, I see Brady standing behind me with his arms crossed.

"No, he's fine," I tell Brady. "Mr. Wallace—"

He cuts me off. "John. Call me John. We're not in the office."

I just want this night to be over with.

"Mr. Wallace, can I drink you—I mean—what can I get you to drink?" I stammer.

That was smooth, real smooth Rose.

Mr. Wallace leans over the table with a come fuck me look, "I'll take Death by Sex."

Oh my fuck!

The women in the office would be lining up to fuck his brains out if they heard him say that.

Keeping me sanity, I write it down. "Gentlemen, I'll be back with your drinks."

I make my way over to the bar to hand it to Felix. Candy approaches me while I'm waiting for table ten's order to be prepared.

"Rose," she says, a little too excited, "you've got a request from a customer for a lap dance."

No fucking way!

"He offered five thousand for fifteen minutes."
Candy's eyebrows wiggle.

Shit, that's good money.

"What do I have to do?" I ask.

"Have you ever pretended to strip in front of an old boyfriend?"

I shake my head. That would be a hard no. "I'm not sure if I could look professional, doing it," I say to her.

"Just wiggle your ass in front of him. He's not allowed to touch you. If he does, your private bodyguard will show him out. We collect the money up front. That way you get paid, if the customer does try to get a little handsy or if anything should happen that is not allowed, we will show him out."

The last thing I want to tell her is that I've only had a five-minute experience in my life. That it was in the dark and it completely sucked, and I wouldn't know what to do with my body if I was given an instructor, but I'm going to leave that out.

"Candy, I'm flattered, but I don't want it. See if someone else would like to earn the money," I tell her.

She seems a little disappointed, but she tries to hide it.

"Okay, but it's a lot of money. Plus, this man asked specifically for you. He's one of our top customers, and he's really picky with whom he wants to dance for him or … other things."

Other things? I can only wonder what that means. "Well, let him down easy then."

She walks off to head to the VIP section.

I know I made the right decision. Stripping and lap dances are not something I want to start doing. I'm not interested in anything else besides waiting on tables.

The night flies by, and it's late when I get off work. I go to the bar to grab my bag. I didn't have time to put it in my locker. I was running a little behind. Feeling tired, I reach in to retrieve my car keys. The inside pocket is empty. Dumping all the contents out of my purse, I frantically look for them.

Brady walks up to me.

"Hey you. Something wrong?"

"I can't find my keys. I know they were in my purse," I reply.

"Let me give you a ride home," Brady offers. "I'm sure they will show up."

I let out a breath of air. He's right. I'm so tired. I'm ready to get home and rest my feet. Hunter has a key to my apartment, so I can just get his key. I need it back anyway.

"I need to make a stop first. I have to get my house key back from my ex."

"Sure thing."

Putting all the contents back into my purse, I slide it on my shoulder.

Brady leads the way to the parking lot. When we stop at the very expensive car, my mouth falls. I'm in complete shock. It's a brand-new Range Rover. How can he afford a ride like this when he's only a bouncer?

I think he notices my shock but doesn't say anything.

I'm about to get in the vehicle when I get slammed

back into something hard. A hand snakes around my waist. Instantly, I know who it is. My body sinks a little into his.

"You're not getting into his fucking truck," Blaze breathes into my ear.

He presses my backside further into him, and he feels so right. I want to close my eyes and inhale him. When he flexes his hips into me, I feel his large friend poking into my backside.

I turn my head to look up at him with my mouth agape. I want to speak, but no words are coming out. Blaze takes the opportunity as an invite; his lips find mine. He kisses me with a fury of passion, sliding his tongue into my mouth. Our lips and tongues are in perfect sync, all while the heat is growing in between my legs. When he pulls away, he eyes Brady and growls.

While I'm still in shock, Blaze picks me up, bridal-style, walking to God knows where. All I can think about is how this man tastes so good. How thick his tongue was. His full but oh-so-soft lips are skillful, more so than any guy I've ever kissed.

I'm coming out of the trance from our kiss when a car door is closed in my face. I'm sitting in something shiny, which is apparently Blaze's vehicle because he's getting in on the driver's side.

This man seriously is fucking with my mind big time.

"What are you doing!" I cry.

"I'm taking you home," Blaze retorts.

What a pain in the ass!

"I could have ridden with Brady."

Blaze stops backing the vehicle up and leans over

to me, and his hand moves up my thigh to cup my sex.

I gasp.

He says in a breathless voice, "NO. ONE. Touches what is mine."

I slap his hand away. "I'm not yours. Get that through that big head of yours!"

I open the car door to escape, but to my disbelief, Blaze reaches over me, slamming it shut.

"If you don't want to be tied up, you won't touch that door handle again. If you want to be tied up … well, go ahead. I'm more than happy to oblige."

He says *go ahead* like it's a threat.

Fuck my life. I feel conflicted by my hormones. I want him, but he's not the relationship type. Yet I can't stop thinking about how good he would look and feel under that shirt that hugs him just right.

No. Rose, stop it. This man is a one-nighter.

5

Blaze

When I open the door at Red and my eyes drank Rose in, my dick took notice of her voluptuous curves. They had me thinking of all kinds of positions to put her in.

Hmm ... the things I want to do to that body.

The way she looked at me, I could tell, I affected her the same way.

My reputation as a playboy has been well-earned. My friend, Wilder, warned me, not to mess around with any of the girls that worked at Red, but being a highly sexually active male, I couldn't resist the temptation.

The women that surround me every day are beautiful, and they make it known that they want to be on my cock. It would be a sin to deny them the pleasure of having a taste. I have no idea how Wilder has so much self-control.

I haven't fucked any of the girls that work at Red in some time. If I get my way—and I always do—Rose will break that streak real soon.

I'm sitting at the bar, watching Rose. Observing all her dark features. She looks like a Greek goddess with medium-length dark hair, olive skin, gorgeous doe eyes, a nice set of large tits, a small waist, and those legs—long, tan, and toned. I want to bury myself in between them. I reach down to rub my erection, not giving two shits who sees me.

When I hear Candy mention to Rose about working a room, something inside of me snaps, making me annoyed as fuck.

Jumping up from my barstool, I stand behind Rose.

"No, she won't be in a room. Only on the floor, waiting tables, nothing more," I command.

She won't be working a room that I made that clear. But the way she defied me, standing up to me, made my dick want to fuck her—hard. I imagine her on top of me, hate-fucking me.

Fuck! I run my hand down my face. I haven't had sex in a couple of days. Pussy is easy for me to get, but the problem is, my dick doesn't want anyone but Rose.

After Rose was taken for a tour, she left for the night. I go to speak to Candy, letting her know I don't want Rose in a room.

"I see her as a better fit for a waitress. She'll begin tomorrow night. Text her." Candy hands me a piece of paper with a phone number on it. "Let her know to be here at five tomorrow. I need her to fill out paperwork." Candy winks at me before walking off.

I text Rose a little later, telling her five o'clock sharp. No reply back. That doesn't surprise me. I grin, knowing she is going to be mine and she doesn't even realize it … yet.

***

The next night, the club is hopping. Being in charge of security, I have been busy trying to make sure all of the girls are safe and we don't have any dumb fuckers trying to give anyone bullshit. Most people don't know that I'm also a silent partner in the business. I leave the books to Wilder. I enjoy the rougher side of the business. There's nothing I prefer more than giving someone a discipline lesson. Tonight is one of those nights.

Spotting a prick in a business suit, I walk a little closer to his table. He's running his sticky fingers up one of the girl's legs, trying to cop a feel. I step to the side of the waitress—Pepper, grab his hand and then give it a hard squeeze. The prick cries out in pain when I feel the break of his fingers, and being the arse that I am, I keep squeezing. I lean down to his ear; I only want to tell him once.

"You're lucky, I only broke your fingers. Keep your fucking hands to yourself unless you are told otherwise."

He doesn't answer. He has his eyes crinkled shut, bending over, trying to deal with the pain. When he does open his eyes, their set on his hand still in my grip. I give him a little initiative to answer my demand by applying more pressure to his already-broken fingers. Finally, I get the response I want. When I release him, he runs out the door. I imagine he's headed to the emergency room.

"Blaze,"—Pepper runs her hands up my chest—"thank you. Can I repay you when I get off work?"

I pull her hand off of me. I've fucked Pepper, but for some reason, her touch makes my skin crawl. I only want Rose's hands exploring my body and only her lips around my cock. I can't stop thinking about her.

After I check with all the girls to make sure there are no problems, I head upstairs to my office. I don't enjoy being in my office. I like being on the floor, where the action is.

I see Rose going toward the storage room, and when she enters, I switch the camera to view the room.

She's so fucking beautiful.

The storage door opens, and it's that shithead, Brady. I instantly jump up from my desk and march downstairs. Brady hasn't been working here long. He started around the same time Rose did, but I get an uneasy feeling about him. I don't like the way he looks at Rose. Now, the dumb fucker is trying to make a move on what's mine. It's time I put an end to this shit.

I open the storage room door with force. Rose is standing in a chair with her legs on display.

Fuck me. I want to take her right now.

Quickly, I focus back on the task at hand—Brady—fucking Brady.

"Brady, didn't I tell you to make yourself useful?

Go keep an eye on the girls up front? Rose doesn't require your attention," I growl.

"He's not bothering me. Thank you for your concern, but you can leave," Rose bites out.

Rose hands a bottle of liquor to Brady, telling him she needs to take it to Felix. When her cheeks turn pink, my rage inflames. I jerk the second bottle out of Rose's hand and push it into Brady's chest.

"Take these to Felix and then get back to your fucking job," I snarl.

When Brady leaves, I wrap my hand around Rose's wrist. When she tries to pull away, I wrap my second hand around her throat. I lean into Rose, pressing my erection into her. I want her to feel how hard she makes me. Bringing my mouth down to her ear, I softly stroke her throat with my thumb. When her eyes flutter, I know she feels something between us too.

"Mo Rós darling," Translation: My darling Rose.

My eyes lock in on her plump heart-shaped lips. I'm moving to taste her perfect lips, when she opens her eyes. She widens them. Rose pushes me off of her and darts out of the room. I stand there a moment, rubbing my straining erection through my jeans.

I know I need to use a different tactic with her than I normally would with any other woman. I want to make her want my cock, just as much as I want her. I leave the storage room, heading back upstairs.

***

It's been a long day and the storage room incident keeps playing over in my mind since Rose walked out last night.

Sitting down at my desk, I glance at the security footage. I'm viewing the footage, making sure everything looks normal and there's no trouble, but my eyes always seem to find Rose, and I can't help the want; growing inside of me. No woman has ever held my interest as she has. There's no doubt that I'm attracted to her, but the need to own and mark her is growing powerful inside of me.

It's the end of the night, and Candy is sitting across from my desk.

"I'm telling you, something is going on with her. Can you just talk to her?" Candy requests.

Candy is concerned about Bonnie. Bonnie has been with our club for some time. A good employee, but she has trouble at home from time to time. She's got shit for taste in men. Whomever she chooses to fuck on her time is none of my concern unless it affects the business.

"Do you feel like it has to do with the club?" I ask her.

"Well … I don't know. I do know this: Bonnie will come to me for anything. She knows my door is always open for her, but she will not talk to me about whatever is going on with her. I don't like it. It makes me think something is wrong."

I groan. "Fine, then I'll speak to her."

"Thanks, Blaze. I know if she feels protected, she'll open up more."

"I'll ask, but if she doesn't want to speak about it, I'm not pushing her."

The last thing I want is for Bonnie to think I want more from her.

Candy gets up and walks out. My eyes go on autopilot when she does, finding Rose on the security footage. She's walking out of the club with fucking Brady.

What is it with this kid? He needs to step the fuck back.

I storm out of my office, making my way to the parking lot. When I see Rose about to get in the SUV with him, I lose my shit. Grabbing her, I pull her with force to my chest.

"You're not getting into his fucking truck," I growl in her ear.

I press her further into me, and when she looks up at me with those rich chocolate eyes and her mouth slightly open, I use this opportunity to show this fucker—Brady— who she belongs too. I press my lips to hers as I guide my tongue in to get a taste. The softness of her lips and the perfect rhythm she moves her tongue with mine make me want more. I want to bed her right fucking now, and if I don't pull away, I will fuck her, owning her body right here in front of everyone.

At the end of our kiss, Rose looks completely bewildered. I glare at Brady, growling. The dumb fuck is watching with a painful look on his face.

Good.

I pick up Rose and start moving to the car. When I put Rose in my vehicle, she doesn't say anything until I get in the driver's seat.

"What are you doing?" she cries out.

"I'm taking you home," I say calmly. I start the car and put it in reverse.

"I could have ridden with Brady," Rose fires back at me.

If she thinks another man will take her home, she's got another thing coming. I stop the vehicle and lean over to Rose, running my hand along her thigh, then cupping her pussy.

"NO. ONE. Touches what is mine."

She slaps my hand and then pushes it away. I smirk. I felt how wet she was. She was soaking wet.

"I'm not yours. Get that through that big head of yours!"

She has no idea.

When Rose reaches over to open the door, I quickly reach over, slamming it shut.

I give her a warning. "If you don't want to be tied up, you won't touch that door handle again. If you want to be tied up … well, go ahead. I'm more than happy to oblige." I say *go ahead* with a sinister look on my face.

Nothing would give me more pleasure than tying Rose up and fucking her sweet cunt till it squeezed my dick coming. I want to hear her as she screams my name while her tight pussy pulses.

My dick doesn't take notice of anyone but her. What the fuck has she done to me? I have no idea. I know one thing, I won't stop till I own every inch of her.

After a brief moment, she slumps back into the car

seat. I'm heading out of the parking lot and turning right when she gives me an address.

"I need to go pick up my apartment key from a friend," she says quietly, staring out of the window.

Confused, I question her, "What? Why would you need to go and get a key from a *friend*?" I emphasize the word *friend*.

Who the fuck is this friend?

"I lost my keys."

She picks up her purse, which looks more like an overnight bag.

"I'm sure I put them in my bag, but I have looked all in here," she says as she fumbles through the overnight bag.

"Hmm." *I need to look at the surveillance cameras.*

I pull up in front of the run-down building. *Who in the living fuck, lives here?* I look at Rose with a stern look.

"Who's your friend that lives here?" I bite out.

She doesn't answer. I can see her lower lip pulled in between her teeth, as if she's contemplating telling me who lives here.

She whispers, "My ex-boyfriend."

Ex-fucking boyfriend!

My possessiveness takes flight. I pull Rose onto my lap. She puts her hands on my chest to push me away, but I wrap my arms around her, pinning her arms down to her sides.

"Mine," I tell her.

"Let me go!" Rose demands.

No fucking way am I letting her go—ever.

"Tell me, what apartment? I'll go get your key."

There's no fucking way I'm letting her out of my sight. Especially to go up to an ex-boyfriend's apartment.

Rose keeps wiggling on my lap, causing my hard shaft to ache to be inside her. I nip at her neck, and Rose lets out a gasp. When she becomes completely still, I start to slowly lick and suck up her neck. I can feel her starting to relax. When I get to her chin, I take it into my mouth and bite down a little as my hands move to grab her perfect, tight round arse. I inhale her scent. Fuck … she smells so good and tastes even better. She gives me more access by tipping her head back. Rose's fingers start running through my hair, grabbing and tugging, while she rocks her hips on my extremely aching dick. Our lips crash, and when I reach up to her full breast, someone honks their horn. In a flash, Rose jumps off my lap, opening the car door.

Fucking hell!

6

Rose

I jump off Blaze's lap. Opening the car door, I escape the small, overheated space. When I run into Hunter's building, the elevator is standing open. I rush to it, frantically pushing the third-floor button. I see Blaze trying to make a dash into the car after me. I push the close button.

Come on, come on.

The doors slide close before he makes it in.

Thank God.

I lean up against the wall, blowing out a breath. I hit myself on the forehead as I think about what just happened.

What was I doing? I started grinding on his dick —his huge dick.

I almost got lost in his lips. If it hadn't been for

someone honking, things would have gone too far. The man knows how to use his mouth. I start imagining how he could put it to use. The elevator comes to a stop, and I get knocked out of big-cock land. I seriously need to stop thinking of his dick. If it were only that simple.

I find myself standing in front of Hunter's apartment. I draw in a slow breath and exhale. I haven't seen him since his sorry excuse of a pecker was in someone's ass. I raise my hand to knock, but I draw it back. My nerves are getting the best of me. I need my house key, so I put on my big-girl panties and knock. The door opens, and Hunter stands in front of me. I look at him. I mean, I really see him.

"Hi," he breathes out.

"Hello," I say, holding my chin up.

"Do you want to come in and talk?" Hunter says hopefully.

"Yes … no I mean, I just got off work and—"

His eyebrows draw up. "Oh … where are you working? Are you not working for the law firm anymore?"

To tell or not to tell. No, he doesn't deserve to know.

"Yeah, I got a part-time job, waiting on tables." Which is not a lie.

"Oh … Rose, I wanted to explain—"

"STOP." I inhale again. I need to try and stay calm. I'm still so angry over what happened. "You don't owe me an explanation. As a matter of fact …" I hesitate, not quite sure of what to say. "I've been seeing someone."

Hunter's eyes go wide.

Yeah, I know. I can't believe I just said that. To

make matters worse, the elevator doors open, and Blaze steps out.

FUCK!

So, what do I do?

"Baby!" I yell to Blaze. "I want you to meet Hunter."

Blaze gives a look of surprise but then displays a cocky grin. To keep Blaze's mouth shut, I stand on my tiptoes to do my best to wrap my arms around his neck—he's so tall. Pulling him down, I quickly give him a peck on the lips.

Whispering in his ear, I warn him, "Keep your mouth shut."

I start to pull away, only Blaze presses me into him while his hand moves down to my ass, squeezing it.

He moans into my neck, loud enough for Hunter to hear.

Dear God, kill me now.

I gently give Blaze a push.

Turning to Hunter, I say, "Hunter, I just came by to pick up my house key."

I give my best smile. The look on Hunter's face is priceless. I should receive an award for my winning performance.

"Hunter." I snap my fingers in his face to wake him out of the daze.

"Yeah … sure."

He reaches into his pocket, pulling out his keys. He pulls off my house key, handing it over. I'm reaching out to take it, but Blaze intercepts, grabbing it.

Pulling me to the elevator, Blaze purrs, "Come on baby. I got something I want to give to you."

I try to hide my face as I roll my eyes.

Yeah, he wants to give it to me and everyone else.

When the elevator doors close, I throw Blaze's hand off of my ass.

"Give me my house key." I glare at him.

He taunts me by dangling it in my face, then reluctantly hands it over.

"I can walk home from here," I say as we exit the car on the first floor.

Blaze follows, but when I walk out of the building, trying to make my way down the sidewalk, Blaze grabs my forearm.

"You're not fucking walking in this shitty neighborhood. Now, get your pretty arse into my fucking car," he says with eyes burning into me.

I would argue with him, but he's right. Hunter lives in a shitty neighborhood, and Blaze looks like he would explode on me if I don't get into his car.

On the ride to my apartment, we don't speak we sit in complete silence. When he pulls up to the front of my apartment complex and stops, I reach for the handle to open the door, but his voice stops me.

"Wait," Blaze commands.

My hand rests on the door handle nervously. When he exits his luxurious sports car, I watch him, not sure what his next move will be. Coming to my door, he opens it.

I didn't expect him to open my door.

Who would have thought a playboy could be a gentleman? The rumors Liz told me about Blaze's playboy ways were not underestimated. The girls in the locker room discuss how he's been with Pepper and other women who are no longer employed at Red. Hell, they even discuss how they want to score with him. I don't want to be just another girl to Blaze, Hunter, or anyone.

Maybe he has some boyfriend qualities that are way down deep that just need to be brought to the surface. Whether he does or doesn't, I don't want to be the one who tries to put their heart on the line, trying to bring those qualities out.

"I'll walk you to your door," he announces.

"It's fine. I—"

"I will walk you, Rose." He speaks with a stern voice.

I nod. I'm too tired to argue with him. I just want to get inside and crash.

When we stop at my apartment door, I clear my throat. "Thank you for the ride," I say quietly as I unlock my door.

He leans on the doorway, smirking. His lips are so close to my ear. I can hear his heart beating, or maybe it's mine. This man makes my heartbeat pick up along with my blood pressure. I don't know whether I'm mad at his playboy ways or if it's the fact that my body wants him.

His lips brush along my ear, causing goose bumps to rise on my skin.

"I'm going to get inside of that pretty, tight little pussy of yours. When I do, you're going to be screaming my name."

He places an open-mouthed kiss on my neck, and a bolt of electricity goes down my spine. His provocative words make my body shiver with want. When he rises, he gives me a smirk of mischief. I'm so shocked by his words and the way my body feels. The only thing that is going through my mind is running. I don't even say a word I quickly open the door and slam it in Blaze's face. I hear him laughing on the other side.

I flop on my couch. My mind is racing with all the events from tonight. How did I lose my keys? And damn Blaze. His mouth is so intoxicating. The way he moves his tongue and his natural dominating ways have me thinking all kinds of dirty thoughts.

No. Rose, don't go there. You will just get hurt.

Speaking of dirty thoughts. I squeeze my eyes shut as I think of Mr. Wallace. Tomorrow, I have to face him. Ugh, it's going to be hell to have to work with him after seeing him at the club.

***

The next morning, I'm scurrying through my office building, doing my best to hurry to get to my desk. I don't want to be anywhere alone with Mr. Wallace, not even for a second. Thankfully, I make it to my chair without running into him. Five minutes later, Liz comes into the office and throws herself into her chair, looking ruffled.

"What the hell happened to you?" I ask Liz.

She rises from her chair and walks over to my

desk, making herself comfortable.

"I had a late night." She rolls her lips.

"Did something happen?"

"Yeah, someone showed up ... unexpectedly."

It's then I see Mr. Wallace exit the elevator. He's looking straight at me as he makes his way over.

Crap.

I busy myself trying to not make eye contact. I start stacking up the folders on my desk. My hands are shaking, making the pile a cluster fuck. The stack of folders falls off the edge of my desk. Papers are flying in the air. I do my best trying to gather all the papers.

Liz looks at me as if I have lost my mind. "What's wrong?" she whispers.

"N-nothing. I'm ... just ..." I'm too stumped to even answer her.

Before Liz can help me gather all the papers, Mr. Wallace puts his briefcase on the floor beside me. I look over to Liz and give her a wide-eyed look. Telepathically requesting Liz for help. She doesn't seem to get the message.

"Rose, are you okay? You look a little pale," Mr. Wallace comments.

I fake a laugh. "Yes, maybe just a little hot."

"I've got to get to work. See you at lunch." Liz waves as she walks off.

What the hell?

Now, I'm stuck here with just me and Mr. Sex On Legs.

I look over to Mr. Wallace just as he licks his lips.

He's looking straight at my chest. I look down to see if maybe I have something on my shirt.

OH NO!

The first couple of buttons are undone, and my breasts are basically hanging out. Quickly, I button up my top.

Mr. Wallace rises, clearing his throat. "Rose, I would like to speak to you in my office when you get done."

Without saying another word, he walks into his office and shuts his door.

After I get the papers put in the right folders, I get up to go see Mr. Wallace. I'm so nervous, and I have no idea what he's going to say.

Knock, knock. I wait for him to say something.

"Come in," he calls.

"Mr. Wallace," I say, looking into the office for him.

He's not seated at his desk. He's seated on the couch. Which makes me a little too uncomfortable. He motions me to sit beside him, but I opt out and take the single chair that is across from the sofa.

"What did you want to see me about?" I wait patiently for his reply.

His face blushes, and I have to admit, he looks so sexy when his cheeks turn pink.

"Rose, I've never … I like to keep my personal life just that—personal. I hope that I can trust you—that what we do outside of work stays there. There's no need to let anyone know of what goes on after work hours."

What is he saying? I'm so out of my realm here.

He sounds like maybe something is happening between us. When, clearly, there's not.

I already want this day to be over and it's just started.

"Of course. Well, if that is all, I need to get back to it."

I walk to his office door, but he's quick to get up and follow after me.

Fuck, just let me leave already.

He moves to stand in front of the door. "Will you be at work tonight?"

"No, I'm off tonight," I tell him, which is yet another lie.

This man might have a beast between his legs, but I'm not interested.

Just move.

His hand reaches up, grabbing me. Panicking, I reach across past him and turn the doorknob. Stevie is standing outside with her fist up in the air, as if she was about to knock on his door. I have never been happy to see her—until now. Mr. Wallace whips his hand off of me, sticking it into his pocket. Stevie must have noticed because she's quick to narrow her eyes.

***

Groaning, I'm hurrying to make it home. I'm late. Mr. Wallace had me doing more transcripts and sending invoices off for him to his clients. I think he was deliberately doing all that shit on purpose because of what happened this morning. I run through my apartment, heading to my room. When Lilly steps out of no-freaking-where with her arms crossed.

"Where are you off to in such a hurry?" Lilly raises an eyebrow.

I pass by her. I don't have time to talk. I need to hurry to get to work. I yell back to her that I need to get ready.

Someone knocks on the door. Thank goodness she leaves me to go and open it.

I hear laughter and wonder who Lilly is talking to. Strapping on my shoes, staggering down the hallway, I want to see what or who has her in such a giddy ball of laughs. I stop as if I have concrete shoes on, weighing me down. Blaze laughs at something Lilly said and looks over at me, gaping. Slowly, he gives me a winning, breathtaking smile.

Why does he have to be so damn hot?

7

Blaze

I let out a laugh when Lilly tells me a story from their childhood. Rose walks into my sight, and I can't help the smile that spreads across my face. Fucking hell, Rose is a walking wet dream in that uniform. A dream that I plan on making a reality.

Rose's eyebrows draw together tightly, "What are you doing here?"

"You were supposed to be at work an hour ago," I bark.

Rose scowls at me.

Lilly looks between us. "Hey, I'm going to hang out tonight while you work. Blaze said he could get me in."

Rose narrows her eyes at me. "Did he now?"

She gives me a shit-eating grin.

She's going to be on my cock in no time.

I smile like the cocky bastard I am. Walking over to Lilly, I wrap my arm around her waist.

I notice Rose's eyes widen.

"I told Lilly I might even buy her a drink," I tease.

I don't plan on giving an underage adult alcohol.

***

When I park the car at Red, I look in the rearview mirror. Rose has her lips drawn tight, her face is red, and she has been staring out of the window since we left her apartment. I told her to grab the backseat so Lilly could sit in the front. Lilly has been talking nonstop. I've laughed at a few things, but to tell the truth, I haven't been listening. The whole ride, my mind was on Rose. I stole glances back and forth between the road and Rose in the rearview mirror.

When we make our way into the club, Lilly looks around in utter shock. Rose is staring at her sister; I can see a battling expression on her face.

"Lilly, let's grab a drink while Rosc gets herself together for her shift."

I try to help out the pain on Rose's face. I imagine Rose hasn't had a discussion with Lilly about what type of bar she works at.

Lilly and I are sitting at the bar. I order a whiskey and Lilly a Coke. When our drinks are placed in front of us, we hear a scream from the back room.

"Fuck!" I yell.

I bolt off my barstool, running at high speed across

the floor to get to the locker room. I know Rose just went back there to put her things up. I'm stricken with worry. My chest hurts from the pounding my heart is giving it. I yank the ladies locker room door open, pulling the handle off, throwing it on the floor.

I mutter, "Piece of shit."

When the door opens, Rose jumps into my arms. Her body is trembling. She's crying, and I'm wondering what the hell is wrong. I pull her back to inspect her body to make sure she's not harmed.

"Rose, baby, look at me. What's wrong?" I say softly.

She looks at me with fear in her eyes, and my determination sets out to kill whoever harmed her. This woman has been in my life for a brief moment, but I know I'll run through fires to keep her safe.

"Rose." I cup her delicate face with the palms of my hands, pulling her to meet my eyes.

She points behind her, and I can't believe it myself. Bonnie's body is hanging from the side of the locker stall. I pull Rose in and stroke the back of her head. She doesn't resist. She wraps her arms around me, fisting my shirt, crying tears into my chest.

This mess needs to be taken care of before word gets out. Dialing Mark, I hear someone gasp. Turning around, I see Lilly standing behind me.

Damn it!

"Turn around and don't say a word," I order Lilly.

I need to keep Lilly from screaming. There's no need in attracting more attention.

She does as I instructed.

"Mark, get down to the ladies' locker room. We have a situation that needs to be cleaned up." I hang up.

I wait on Mark. This problem could get out of hand if it's not kept under wraps.

Mark walks into the locker room with his dick almost hanging out of his pants.

"Fuck man, zip your fly. I can see your hairy dick."

Fucking hell. The last thing I want is Rose looking at another man's dick. The only cock she's going to see is the one in my pants. It's just a matter of time before she knows she's mine.

I nod to Bonnie's lifeless body.

"Fuck!" Mark says under his breath.

I'm still holding on to Rose while keeping an eye on Lilly.

"We need to call Wilder." I move my eyes to Rose.

Mark looks at Lilly and then speaks in our native language.

"Faigh amach as seo iad. Glaofaidh mé ar Wilder agus tabharfaimid aire don chorp." Translation: Get them out of here. I will call Wilder and we'll take care of the body.

I guide the girls out the back door, and we get into my car. Lilly doesn't say a word, and Rose has her head buried in her hands all the way to her apartment. When we finally make it up to her apartment door, Rose's hand is shaking so bad that she's not able to get the key into the lock. I take the key, unlocking the door. Lilly rushes to a bathroom, and I hear her upchucking. Rose looks pale and doesn't move from her spot in front of the doorway.

I lift Rose in my arms. "Which one is your bedroom?"

She slides her hands up, interlocking her arms around my neck.

"Straight down the hallway," Rose whispers.

Entering the room, I notice the plush comforter that is on her bed with a dozen pillows. I bend to lay Rose down, retreating back to stand straight. Rose doesn't let go of me. I look into her eyes that have swelled from all the tears she has shed.

I forget how innocent others can be. Seeing death doesn't affect me. I have been hard from a very young age.

When I was a young lad, I was playing in the neighbor's yard when I heard gunshots. My stomach rolled over with a feeling of uneasiness that something was wrong. I ran home and into our back door. Indeed, something was wrong. I spotted my parents, lying in their own puddle of blood that coated the carpet. My parents were dead on the living room floor, and from that moment on, I changed. My heart hardened I was determined to make sure I never felt that vulnerable again. Losing my parents that day took me over to the dark side.

I've been investigating their death ever since. No one knows who committed their murder—or at least they're not talking. I never saw anyone come into the house that day, nor did I see anyone leave. My parents were loved by everyone. I can't imagine who would commit such a crime against such a loving couple.

"Don't go." Rose looks up at me with pleading eyes.

I begin pushing her hair behind her ears. "Let me go

check on Lilly. I'll be back."

Fuck! This is a complete clusterfuck! Who in their right fucking mind would pull a stunt, killing one of our girls? I'm going to enjoy slowly killing someone piece by piece.

I bang on the bathroom door.

"Lilly." I'm about to speak again, but she opens the door.

"I'm okay. Just going to lie down."

I nod. Walking into Rose's room, I shut the bedroom door. She turns to me, watching me as I slip my shirt over my head and slide my shoes off. I crawl up the bed toward her, and she spreads her legs for me. I know this isn't the time to fuck her senseless because she's completely fragile, but fuck, I want to ram my cock in her so bad that it's aching to feel her warmth.

"Rose," I whisper into her lips as I kiss them tenderly.

She hums as her hands slide up my bareback.

I deepen the kiss by plunging my tongue into her mouth as I press my hard cock into her sex. I slide my tongue over hers, and it feels so right. When I pull back to thrust my hips into her sex again, she stops me by wrapping her legs around my waist.

Fuck! I need to stop this. I don't want to take advantage of her state of mind.

I pull my lips away from hers. Only being centimeters apart, I breathe the air she breathes out. We stare into each other's eyes, and when I'm about to dive back in for another kiss, my cell rings.

I don't want to look away from the beautiful sight in

front of me, but I know I need to get back to taking care of Bonnie's body.

Picking my phone out of my pants, I click the Answer button, "Yeah?"

Wilder barks into the phone. "Put your dick in your pants and get your arse back here. We have got a fucked up situation that shouldn't have happened in the club."

Fucking hell. I look at the beautiful woman under me. Her eyes are set on me. I can see how scared she is. I hang the phone up without saying good-bye. I lean down to brush my lips one more time against Rose's.

"I have to go," I whisper into her lips. "Stay up for me. I'll be back as quickly as I can."

She blinks.

"No." That is all she says.

I raise an eyebrow. "No what?"

"No, you shouldn't come back. This was … was a mistake. We shouldn't be doing this. I'm just in complete shock over seeing Bonnie."

Mo Rós darling, I'm not giving you a choice." I grin. "Don't speak to anyone about what happened tonight. Punishment will be severe if you do."

She swallows hard.

I know this is a lot for someone to process. The kind of people we deal with are not always the most upstanding citizens. Some of the men we run into are dangerous and will do anything or kill anyone who crosses the wrong path with them. Until we have an idea of who we are dealing with, she needs to stay quiet.

I make my way off the side of the bed, putting my

shirt and shoes back on. I reach for her bedroom door handle, stopping, and I turn back to Rose. "Open the door for me, or I'll make my own way in." I walk out shutting the door a little too hard.

I decide to peek in on Lilly as I walk down the hallway. I want to make sure she is okay. When I open her bedroom door, I see she is lying on her side, facing away. Closing the door, I leave out of the front apartment door.

***

Upon my arrival at Red, I walk into Wilder's office.

"About fucking time you got back!" Wilder yells.

Not speaking, I sit in the chair beside Mark. Mark has a shit-eating grin on his face. Fucking hell. I don't need shit from him. I know he's fucking someone at the club. He's very secretive about who it is, but it's only a matter of time till we find out.

Wilder throws something across his desk at me.

Catching it, I look at the red rose charm on the key ring.

"Mark says you might have an idea of whose key chain that is," Wilder comments.

I stuff the keys in my pocket and nod. "I'll take care of it. Where did you find them?" I ask.

"They were on the floor beside the bar," Wilder replies. "Mark took Bonnie's body and disposed of it. It looks as if someone hung her. There's no way she did that herself. The dumb arse didn't even bother putting a stool close to her to make it look like she hung herself." Wilder runs his hand through his hair. "The last thing we want is cops snooping around."

Looking at Mark, I ask, "Where did you take the body?"

Mark replies, "Her house. Set it up to look like she committed suicide."

"Blaze, look at all the security footage and see who was coming in and out of that locker room. I can't believe this fucking shit happened here." Wilder slams his fist down.

"On it, boss." I head out to my office.

Sitting down at my computer, I bring up the security footage, examining the videos for the whole day. I finally see where Bonnie goes into the locker room, and then the security camera time jumps exactly thirty minutes later.

FUCK! This is not good. It seems that this could be an inside job.

Noticing the time, I turn the computer off before I leave. I see Wilder's still in his office. Standing in his doorway to his office, I see him deep in thought while he's looking at his laptop.

"I'm out for the night," I tell him.

He looks up and throws me a head tip.

I want to head back over to Rose's. When I open the back door to leave, Brady jumps in surprise.

"Shit!" Brady screams like a bitch.

He seems awful jumpy. I narrow my eyes at him.

What the hell is he doing out here in the first place?

"What the fuck are you doing?" I bark at him.

"I … I had to make a personal phone call," Brady retorts.

"Get your arse inside and do your damn job."
I watch him as he heads inside.
Stupid fucker.

8

Rose

I'm lying on my bed, looking up at the ceiling. Every time I close my eyes, I see Bonnie hanging from the side of the stall. Her eyes open, looking in the direction of the locker door.

Oh God. I turn and sob into my pillow. Poor Bonnie. I knew she had trouble, but I can't imagine what caused her to commit suicide. I can't imagine it could be that bad.

My door opens, and I expect it to be Lilly, I look up to see Blaze. He's standing in my bedroom doorway, eyes trailing over my body. I'm lying on top of the duvet in a camisole and a lace thong. His chest is rising and falling in a fast rhythm.

Shit, I thought I had locked the door when he left.

I quickly try to wrap the coverlet around me, but Blaze's words stop me.

"DON'T," he breathes out.

He closes the door and stalks over to me. My heart is racing, Should I run, or do I allow myself the pleasure of his hard body pressing into me? Before I have time to process my thoughts, Blaze scoops me up in his arms. I'm so transfixed on his beautiful face; I can't speak or look away. He walks to the adjacent bathroom and stands me on the cold tiled floor. I'm facing him, and our eyes are locked on each other.

"Turn around," Blaze orders me.

I turn around, and his hand grabs the hem of my camisole.

Kissing my neck softly, he says, "Raise your arms."

When I do, he slides the camisole over my head, letting it drop to the floor. I hear him growl in appreciation at the sight of my ass. When I feel a sting on my ass cheek, I whip my head around to see a perfect handprint.

"Turn around," Blaze says with a rugged voice.

He looks as if he's struggling to keep calm.

Before I can turn completely around, he slaps my opposite ass cheek. It stings, but the pain feels erotic.

Once I'm turned again, I do as I was told, waiting to see what he will do next.

His strong, callous hands roam down my back, making their way to my ass. His hands squeeze a handful of my ass. I hear him unzip his pants and the rustle of clothes being dropped to the floor. I close my eyes as the heat in my core heightens. I'm on edge, needing his hands to touch me. As quickly as the thought occurs, his hands glide over my hips, passing my panty line, and they stop at the neatly shaved strip of hair. He sucks in a breath, then locks his lips on my earlobe.

"Fuck, Rose, your body is all I can think about."

His words have me panting.

"Touch me, Blaze. I need you to touch me."

"Tell me … tell me how you want me to touch you."

I feel my cheeks heat up. I'm not a dirty talker. I've only been with one boy, and I was so much younger. Blaze is completely out of my sexual experience league.

"Tell me, Rose, where do you want me to touch you?" Blaze licks my neck, causing an electric shock to start in my pussy.

I take his hand that is on my manicured pubic hair and try to push it down to my swollen clit, but he resists.

"Words, Rose. I want you to say it," Blaze demands.

I swallow the dry lump in my throat. "Pussy … touch my pussy."

His middle finger slides into my lips, over my clit, and dips into me as his other fingers cup my pussy.

"Fuck, you're so wet," he breathes in my ear.

He pushes his finger deep inside, causing me to moan out loud. He starts slowly moving in and out of me. When his breathing picks up, his finger starts fucking me hard while the palm of his hand hits my clit. I'm a mess trying to hold myself up. I grip his arms as I scream out my release. My body spasms around his finger. When I stop convulsing, I breathe heavily, leaning up against him.

Blaze brings his fingers to my lips. "Open."

I obey.

"Good girl. Now suck," he growls into my ear.

I feel his hard cock against my backside.

"Get in the shower and on your knees."

Huh? When did he turn on the shower?

There's a knock at the door, and I snap into a panic. My eyes go wide. Blaze is now standing in the shower with a very impressive-looking cock in his hand. I'm frantically looking around, trying to find my camisole.

"Looking for this?" Blaze asks with a cocky grin.

Holding out my hand, I whisper, "Give it to me."

"Do what you're told. I'm not done fucking you." He smirks.

"Fucking hell! I'll just walk out of here with nothing but my thong," I puff out.

"Rose, are you okay? I heard you screaming," Lilly yells from the other side of the bathroom door.

I holler back, "Yeah … just a bug."

When I hear the bedroom door shut, I know she won't be back.

I reach up on my toes to retrieve my top from Blaze. Instead, he pulls me into the shower, then throws my camisole out of reach. Placing the palms of his hands on both sides of my face, he draws me closer, and his lips softly brush mine, spiring into a kiss. The kiss is soft and passionate. Something that I would have never expected from him. It's breath takingly good. His hands move down to my neck and onto my shoulders. He breaks the kiss, pushing down on my shoulders.

"Get on your knees," he commands.

I lower myself on the shower tiles without breaking eye contact. His hand cups the side of my face as his other hand gives his length slow strokes.

"Mo Rós darling, I plan on fucking every part of you. Your beautiful tits, arse, and pussy are mine, only mine. Now, press your tits together. When I come, I'm going to cover them, declaring them mine."

This new sexual feeling is all-consuming. I want to make him wilt in my hands. So, I do something that I would have never thought about doing before. I grab my tits and push them together, and then I make eye contact with Blaze. Sticking out my tongue, I do my best to lick my way down my breast to my nipple.

"I'm ready … Daddy."

"Fuck me," Blaze says with hooded eyes as he strokes his dick harder.

He positions his hard cock in the midst of my double-Ds and takes my breast for a fast and rough ride. When he is about to come, he pulls out.

"Open your pretty mouth."

He throws his head back as his cum releases onto my chest, neck and inside of my mouth. Drawing his eyes back to meet mine, he swipes his thumb across my lips putting it into my mouth.

"Taste what you do to me."

Closing my lips around his thumb, I suck while I swirl my tongue, making sure to get every drop off.

After Blaze washes me off ever-so gently, I'm barely able to keep my eyes open. I have been well and truly finger-fucked like nothing I've experienced before, and my mental state of mind from early this evening has made me debilitated.

***

The next morning, I wake up to an empty bed. Scooping up my robe, I wrap it around me. Still having sleep in my eyes, I walk into the kitchen, gathering everything I need to make coffee.

Lilly stops in the doorway with her suitcase in tow.

"What are you doing? You're not supposed to leave for another day."

Lilly's face looks pale. "I'm leaving. Last night really startled me. I'm ready to go back to my bubble, where I don't see dead bodies."

She drops her bags, and walks over to me, wrapping me into a tight hug.

I pull her back, "Do you want me to drive you?"

"No, I called a taxi. I didn't want to disturb you." Facing me, she asks, "Promise me, Rose, you will stop working there. That place doesn't give me good vibes."

I nod because there's no need for her to worry.

"Please don't talk to anyone about what we saw yesterday. I don't want to get either one of us into trouble."

I thought Bonnie hung herself, but with Blaze telling me not to speak to anyone, I'm not sure what to think.

"At least let me walk you out," I plead.

When I get back to my apartment, my door is unlocked. I know I locked it. Easing into my apartment, I listen for anything out of the ordinary. After searching the whole apartment, I let out a long breath. The scene I saw with Bonnie yesterday has got me in a nervous state.

***

Several hours later in the evening, I can still feel myself walking on cloud nine, reminiscing on last night's physical activities.

Blaze hasn't contacted me today. I imagine he had prior engagements to attend to—at least, I'm hoping that's the reason he hasn't contacted me today. I do my best to push out thoughts of him only wanting one thing from me.

Getting dressed for work, I am beyond nervous and excited to see him tonight. My mind hasn't shut off thinking about last night. How sexy he was, stroking himself. His body truly looks like it was carved by the gods.

I look at myself in the mirror. I've put on a bra that pushes my girls up. Spraying my hair one more time, I turn to check out my ass.

Not bad.

I have put in a little more effort tonight, hoping Blaze will take notice. I'm not a skinny girl. I have curves. I've always had boobs and a butt. I developed earlier than most of my friends, and it took me some time to be comfortable with my body. Once I became more confident, the guys took notice. After checking myself out one more time, I head out to work.

***

Once I'm at Red, I get started on my tables. We are packed tonight. There must be a special event going on because I've never seen it this busy before.

I haven't seen Blaze all night—until now. I take a deep breath because I want to go and rip his ass a new one. He's sitting at the bar, looking a little too cozy with Pepper. Her hand is crawling up his chest, and he doesn't bother to remove it. She must be telling him something awfully funny because he's laughing like she's the best comedian he's ever heard.

I throw my towel down. *That ass!*

Candy comes over to my side, telling me someone has requested a lap dance from me.

"Is this the same man?" I ask her.

"No, but he's very persistent that he wants you," she smiles.

"Yes, I'll do it. The same amount of money, right? Five thousand?"

"Yes."

"Please, lead the way!" I smile from ear to ear.

Candy gives me a uniform the girls wear when they do lap dances. It's a little too little. Almost leaving nothing to the imagination. I fumble with the tiny top and bottom, trying to make sure all my girl parts are covered. I'm not sure if this is my size. I think I need a bigger size, but Candy insists this is the correct size.

I stand in the hallway, taking deep breaths, trying to

calm my nerves. The door that leads to my customer is in front of me. Brady is supposed to be my bodyguard for this dance. I haven't seen him, so I'm hoping he's waiting for me inside. I take my last deep breath and walk into the room.

My face scrunches up. "What are you doing here!"

Hunter is sitting with a drink in his hand, smiling at me.

"I want my lap dance … whore," he slurs.

I turn to leave because this is not happening.

Hunter gets up and grabs my wrist, gripping it painfully. I raise my free hand in a motion to slap him but he catches it. Looking around, I don't see Brady in the room.

Just my luck!

A loud noise occurs. I'm struggling to try to break loose of Hunter's tight hold when suddenly, he's thrown to the other side of the room. I feel as if I'm in a slow-motion film as Blaze picks Hunter up off the floor, repeatedly slamming his fist into his face. I stand, horrified at the scene happening.

Completely stunned at Hunter being here and pissed at Blaze for the way he allowed Pepper's hands to roam his chest, I stand still until my heavy feet feel light enough to pick up and walk out of the room.

I make it halfway down the hallway before I'm lifted into the air and tossed over a shoulder. Inhaling the familiar cologne, I start punching Blaze's back. I don't want him anywhere near me.

He walks into an unoccupied room and throws me on the bed.

"Get away from me," I yell, trying to jump off the bed.

He doesn't bother to answer me. Unbuckling his belt, he gives me a dark warning with a shaking of his head. He whips his belt out of the pant loops. Folding it in half, he cracks it.

"Don't fucking move. I warned you not to let another man touch you."

"Don't you dare touch me with that." I point to his belt.

Before I know it, Blaze has pulled me down the bed and flipped me onto my stomach. Kicking and screaming are not helping me to get loose from his hold. It's then I feel a sharp pain and hear a loud crackling sound. It's the first strike he's taken across my ass. It's painful, but he doesn't stop after the first one. There's a second and a third. I cry, lying on my stomach. When he stops, I hear the belt being dropped on the hardwood floor.

"Roll over." His command is threatening.

When I roll over, I bite my lip from crying out loud. The stinging of my ass is agonizing.

Blaze's eyes are dark, and I can see the outline of the hardness in his pants. He leans down, possibly to kiss me, but instead he takes his hands and forces my bloomers down, dragging my underwear with them.

A tear runs down the side of my face.

"I'm going to fuck you so hard; you'll know that I am the only one you're allowed to touch. That my cock will be the only one you're allowed to suck. You belong to me, *Mo Rós darling.*"

"I don't belong to anyone," I spit back.

"Close that pretty mouth of yours before I gag you with my cock … darling."

9

Blaze

I look down at the neatly trimmed strip of hair on Rose's pussy. I'm hard—so fucking hard. My dick is completely throbbing with want.

Remembering Rose this morning, lying completely naked, looking so peaceful while she slept, made me want to wake up to that sight every day.

If I didn't have prior engagements to meet with the Anderson twins this morning, I would have stayed in her bed to ravish her pussy with my tongue and cock all day.

"Are you wet for me, Mo Rós darling?"

"No!" she barks.

Giving her a wicked grin, I push Rose's knees up to her shoulders, then spread her legs. Her sweet cunt is glistening.

Fuck, so sweet.

Not wanting to wait any longer to be inside of her, I grab her off the bed and back her against the wall. Positioning my arms under her thighs, I raise her into the air and slam her down on my cock, thrusting my hips to make sure to bury myself completely inside her. She arches her back, letting out a scream as my cock fits snugly into her tight pussy.

I moan from her slick heat choking my shaft.

"Fuck yes," I say with hooded eyes.

Rose holds onto my shoulders, as I begin to bounce her on my dick. Her sweet heat starts to squeeze my shaft.

I command, "Don't fucking come until I say you can."

Her eyes go wide, and she slaps me across the face.

"Don't fucking let other women touch you," she fires at me.

I throw her onto the bed, pulling her up onto her knees. Positioning the thick head of my cock at her entrance, I push in full throttle.

I slap her arse. "Don't ever fucking think you will give anyone a lap dance, but me."

She whimpers. I know it stings from the arse beating I gave her earlier. I couldn't control my anger. Seeing her leaving with Candy made something in me go primal. When I saw Candy escort Rose down the hallway, I knew she had been requested again for a lap dance. What I didn't know was that it was by her fucking ex-boyfriend.

"Shut the hell up and just fuck me," Rose demands.

I pull out of her, tossing her on her back. I crawal up her body. She looks at me with heat in her eyes.

"I warned you to shut that pretty mouth."

I reach back to her swollen clit and pinch it. When she opens her mouth to let out a gasp, I shove my cock in.

"Suck. If you bite, you won't be prepared for the punishment."

Leaning up on the headboard, I start to ride Rose's face.

"Fuck … take all of my cock," I grit out.

I push all the way into Rose's mouth. She takes me like she was made to suck my dick.

With a sharp intake of air, I say, "Fucking hell."

My balls are about to burst up in flames.

Rose does something unexpected; she slaps me on the arse and then reaches around to cup my balls.

I'm about to lose it.

I pull out of her mouth. Looking at her, I say, "Are you going to be a good girl?"

Her eyes are full of desire. "No."

Shoving my cock back into her mouth, I run my fingers into Rose's hair, balling a fistful, while I push my cock farther down her throat. I'm only satisfied when I feel Rose's nose pushed up against my skin.

Fuck yes, I just want to keep my dick buried in her —happily buried in her mouth, pussy, or arse. I don't give a shit.

She works her tongue around my shaft as I slowly push back. I'm so ready to fuck her.

When I pull out of her mouth, our eyes meet.

"Are you going to be a good girl?"

She swallows. "Good girl … yes … Daddy."

I roll my eyes back, hearing her call me that.

I've lost all ability to be gentle when I crawl down Rose's body.

"I can't be gentle; I need to fuck you hard."

I flip her over onto her stomach and pull her up back to her knees. Grabbing my aching cock, I slide it along her wet heat.

Needing to be inside of her like my lungs need air, I ask, "You ready for me, *Mo Rós darling?*"

Before she can answer, I plow into her sweet pussy with a single hard thrust.

Ever since I opened the door at Red, I've been hard for Rose and only Rose.

I rise to my feet on the bed, still having my cock buried in her sweet heat I drive into her, each thrust becoming harder. My balls slap up against her pussy, causing an unbelievable vibration.

Fuck.

When I feel her sweet cunt squeeze, I pull out. She looks over her shoulder at me with a whimper. Drawing back, I look down at the wetness dripping down her thighs. Leaning down, I run my tongue up her thigh, getting a taste.

She shivers.

"Fuck baby, you taste so sweet."

My dick is still slick from her sweetness. Aligning myself up with her little dark back hole. I start to push in. Rose whips her head around and tries to fall forward. I grab her hips to hold her still.

"Don't—" she cries.

I push into her, closing my eyes in ecstasy.

"Fuck yes!" I hiss out.

Rose squeezes her arse.

Reaching around to her clit, I massage it.

"Relax baby. Shh. Relax."

She tried to protest at first, but the pleasure takes over, and she relaxes. I pull back and push in, not quite taking her hard. I can tell she's never been fucked in the arse before, and something inside of me comes alive, knowing I'm the only one that's ever entered here. I want her I want whatever she comes with. I'll kill anyone who thinks they can take *Mo Rós, darling*. She's mine. All fucking mine.

***

After having Rose twice. I go into the en-suite and gather a wet cloth. Coming back to her, I whisper into her ear, "Roll over, *Mo Rós darling*."

She does as I asked. Once I'm finished cleaning her, I start picking up her clothes to dress her. She tries to disapprove, but I give her a warning.

"I'm driving you home."

"I still have to work the rest of my shift."

I look at her, taking in her angelic face.

"No, you won't be working here anymore."

She rises so quickly. I could have sworn her head spun around.

A fierce look appears on her face. "I didn't ask you, and you don't tell me what to do."

"Don't fight me on this, Rose. You won't like the outcome," I yell.

Rose snatches what's left of her clothes out of my hand. She finishes dressing and makes an effort to leave the room, but I step in front of her with crossed arms.

"Move," Rose commands.

"You're not going back out there to work." I stand my ground.

The thought of other men trying to make a move on her has my blood rushing through my veins like lava.

I've fucked other girls who have worked at Red, not giving a shit if they fuck anyone else. That's not the case with Rose. I'll crush anyone who tries to touch her. She's mine, only mine.

"Listen to me … Blaze." She spits my name out. "You or any other man will not tell me what to do. I'm not someone you can just push around." She does her best effort to push me out of the way.

"I. NEED. THIS. JOB!"

"You're going home tonight." I fire back.

I swing low and pick her up, placing her on my shoulder. I walk out of the room and out of Red with her claws in my back.

***

We arrive at her apartment. Opening the passenger door, I lift Rose. I had to tie her in the car because she kept trying to open the fucking car door. She's like a fierce kitten. Not taking shit from me. Thinking about my little kitten makes my dick hard.

Once I lift her out of the car, Rose punches me in the arse the complete ride up to her apartment.

When we get off the elevator, I smack Rose's arse. "Behave."

She finally stops fighting me. I exhale, setting her down on the floor. It's then I notice her apartment door is open.

What the fuck!

When I glance at Rose, I see she notices it too, seeming as equally surprised as I am.

When I start to untie her, I whisper in her ear, "Is your sister here?"

She shakes her head.

"Stay here," I order.

I pull out my gun and cock it. I walk into her apartment, and Rose follows me in. I turn to give her a death glare.

I whisper, "Didn't I tell you to fucking stay outside?"

She gives me a small grin as she puts a death grip on the tail of my shirt.

Fucking hell. This woman is infuriating.

After checking all the rooms, we come to the half-open door that leads to Rose's bedroom. Pushing it open, I see it's a complete disaster area. All of her underclothes have been pulled out, shredded lying everywhere on the bed. Her clothes from the walk-in closet have been pulled out and are lying on the floor. I smell a faint scent of gas in the air. Moving closer to the pile of clothes, a door slams, causing Rose to jump. Her arms wrap around me from behind.

I do my best to race in the direction of the sound, but Rose is holding onto me too tight, and I'm not able to get to it in time. How the hell someone slipped pass me. I have no fucking idea.

Looking at Rose's face, I can tell she is completely shaken.

"Hey." I cup her face, pulling her up to meet my gaze.

"It's okay. I'm here."

10

Rose

If Blaze thought I was staying behind, he had another thing coming. I pride myself on being a strong woman, but there are times I'm willing to admit, I'm completely scared shitless.

"Thank you," I whisper.

With shaky hands, I reach around Blaze. I just want his hard oversize body to engulf me till I wake up from this nightmare.

Reaching down, Blaze strokes my face with his large, powerful hands.

"I want you to calm down and think about who would want to do this?" His bold sapphire eyes bore into mine, searching for answers. "Is there anyone that comes to mind?"

I scrunch my face. *Who would have done this intentionally ... to me?*

I reply, "I can't think of anyone. Maybe they have me confused with someone else."

Blaze pulls his phone out of his pocket, dialing a number. He speaks in his native language. His voice is harsh, loud, and the look on his face is one that would scare King Kong. When he hangs up, he grabs my hand, almost dragging me out of the apartment.

"What are you doing?"

He stops, turning to me. His eyes are dark, a storm brewing behind them, causing me to flinch. He steps closer, crowding me.

His voice is gruff when he speaks. "Do you think I will leave you here for whoever to come back to harm what's mine?"

I would disagree with him that I'm not his if I wasn't so fearful of the rage that is seeping from him. Instead, I stand quietly till he tugs at my hand, leading the way out of my apartment.

Blaze doesn't speak to me until we make it to his car. Even then, he basically yells at me to get into the car when he opens the door for me.

Taking a seat, I watch Blaze as he walks over to crawl into the driver's seat. God, he's so intense. He's also sexy, dominating, and aggravating as hell, but damn, he's completely intoxicating. The way he punished me with his cock has me all kinds of squirming in my seat.

***

When he turns into an underground parking lot, he comes to a stop when he pulls up to the elevator. Blaze gets out of the car. A man steps out of the shadows, appearing on my side. Blaze greets him.

When Blaze opens my door, I tell him, "Thank you."

He pulls my sweaty, small palm into his warm, large hand. The size difference between us is remarkable, but the feel of his hand sends tingles straight up my spine. It feels almost like … no, it's completely just sex. Yes, just sex.

Once we are in the elevator, I see the man get into the driver's seat and drive off before the elevator doors close. When we reach our floor and the doors open, a breathtaking view of city lights comes into sight. It's amazing! I step out onto a floor that I can see my reflection on. Walking to the glass wall, I place my hand on it. The glass is cool to the touch. From the view, I can see small dots of light zooming beneath us. I wonder how many stories are beneath us. Blaze walks up to me, leaning down, I hear him inhale my hair.

"I'm having your locks changed on your apartment."

I take in a deep breath and exhale. He's being … protective. Something inside me tightens. What if he feels obligated because of what happened to Bonnie? What if he slept with her and feels the need to protect me because he doesn't want to see my lifeless body in the locker room? There are too many what if's and now, my head is starting to swirl from all the thinking.

"I'd like to grab a shower and go to bed," I breathe out.

"Come."

We walk through Blaze's penthouse. There's no color on the walls, floors, or even the furniture. Everything is white with no personality, no sign that life exists here. The bedroom is the same—no personality. When the motion lights come on in the bathroom, it's the first sight of color other than white. Black marble countertops, and the same marble is in the shower.

Blaze turns the shower on and reaches down to grab my shirt.

"I can undress." I try to push his hand away, but it's no use. Giving up, I let him undress me.

Once he successfully undress me, his eyes roam my body.

Blaze's eyes burn into me. "Get in."

When I step into the shower, the warm water feels so good on my aching muscles. Not feeling his presence behind me, I wipe the water from my eyes. Blaze stands against the marble countertop with his pants unzipped and his wide length fisted in his hand and his gaze fixed on me.

"Wash your breasts with your hands."

Seeing him stroke himself while he soaks me in makes me what to please him.

Doing as he said, I lather up my hands with the bar of soap. Placing them on the underside of my breasts. I slowly work them up, stalling over my nipples. I grasp them between my thumbs and forefingers tugging at them.

Hearing Blaze take a sharp breath in, I glance over

at him. His eyes are completely dark, and they're set on me. Feeling this new power over him, I close my eyes and then slide one hand down to my sex, slowly rubbing my clit.

It's then I'm pushed up against the tile wall. He lifts my leg, positioning his large girth at my entrance.

He whispers into my ear, "Mine."

His thrust is forceful as he fills me, making my body aware of his invasion. He grunts into my ear as he takes what he wants from me.

My breathing comes out in short breaths as he fucks me against the wall. The pleasure and the pain mixing together, it's too much. I start to feel my body teeter on the edge of an orgasm.

"Don't stop. Feels … feels so good," I gasp out as my nails dig into his back.

Blaze's thrusts become harder, and his grunts become louder. Holding onto his shoulders, I completely fall, riding the waves of an orgasm, being lost in the pleasure. My body shakes out the aftershocks of a powerful climax.

He thrusts, one more time pushing himself further into me. I feel his release, the pulsing of his shaft, throbbing inside of me. His hips are still as his head drops onto my shoulder.

Our heartbeats are in sync with a steady rhythm as they come back down from the height of falling.

He looks … beautiful, panting into my skin. When his eyes open, I catch sight of an emotion behind those hypnotizing blues, a yearning, a burning in them. I'm overtaken, speechless at how this man who's so stunning, who can have anyone wants me. As soon as he blinks, the desire is gone.

Feeling foolish for having such a thought I let him pull out of my body. We take turns in bathing each other, then drying off,

"I need some clothes."

"Just a moment."

Blaze walks out of the bathroom and returns with a shirt. When I pull it over my head, I inhale a large intake of air. God, his scent is so strong on the shirt.

We silently walk into the bedroom, where Blaze has the covers drawn.

"You need to rest," he says as he guides me to the side of the bed.

Lying on the soft, plush mattress that's covered with silk sheets, I instantly fall asleep.

***

I peek through slits in my eyes, seeing daylight. Closing my eyes completely, I try to roll over to rise, but something is weighing me down. Blaze is lying with an arm and a leg draped over me. I wiggle around to take in a closer view. I thought he looked beautiful last night, but seeing him lying here, so peaceful, his thick, long eyelashes fanning over his face. His lips are full they would make any woman envious. This man was carved by the gods themselves.

His eyes flutter open, and a small smile displays on his full lips.

With a raspy voice, he whispers, "Good morning, *Mo Rós darling.*"

My stomach does a little flip at hearing that rough voice.

"Morning," I whisper back.

He rolls onto his back, giving me a good view of his strong chest. I run my fingers between his pecs, admiring the perfection of his physique.

"I'm going to fix breakfast, and then I'm going to fuck you again. You need strength for what I have planned." He gives me a wink and then rolls out of the bed.

11

Rose

After the wide spread of breakfast Blaze fixed and another round of some hard-core wrestling between the sheets, I asked him to take me home. He tried to keep me pinned under him, but eventually, I won the argument.

I head inside my apartment with the new key Blaze gave me. Making my way down the hallway to my bedroom, I stop at the doorway, taking in the tidy room. Nothing out of sorts, no ripped underclothes, no clothes lying on the floor. Everything has been cleaned up.

I wonder …

Walking into my closet, I blink. There are new clothes lined neatly on all three of the clothing rods.

What the every living crap!

Pulling my cell out of my back pocket, I dial Blaze.

He answers without speaking. I can tell he's there because I hear his breathing.

"Why did you get rid of my clothes and replace them with new ones? I can't afford these." I yell at him.

"*Thank you*—that's what most people say when you do something nice for them. And, no, you won't be paying me back. I can afford it."

I take a moment to meditate before I speak because I know he's right. It was nice of him, and I do appreciate it, but I was caught off guard.

Blowing out a large breath of air, I reply, much nicer, "Thank you, but I don't think us sleeping together is a need for you to spend"—I twirl my hand up in the air—"all this money. It wasn't necessary."

A low growl comes through the line. "Darling." The word comes out of his lips, thick with venom. "You're MINE. You need to realize that I own you. I will take care of you and your needs."

"No one owns me, Blaze."

He laughs. His laugh contains a darkness in it that sends shivers up my spine. I know the world he lives in, is much different from the crisp white apartment he sleeps in. It's a world filled with guns, murder, sex, and whatever else lurks in dark alleys.

All of a sudden, I feel vulnerable. I don't like feeling this way. I could say again that no one owns me, but I'm afraid of how weak it might sound.

Doing my best to sound strong, I tell Blaze. I'm not an object. Then, quickly, I end the call.

As I stand in the middle of my closet, realization

spreads through me. I know being with Blaze will cost me in the end.

***

After a shower, I give Liz and Vinnie a call, asking if they want to meet to grab a bite.

Walking into the café, I spot Liz sitting at a table. She's texting and doesn't notice me until I pull out my chair.

"Liz."

She glances up, and immediately, her face blushes. I raise my brows.

Sitting down, I say, "Something interesting happening on your phone?" .

She waves me off.

"Did you know that Vinnie is seeing Cynthia?" Liz says with a sour look on her face.

"Who's Cynthia?"

Tilting her head, she says, "You know, the blonde bimbo at the receptionist's desk."

"Oh, her, I didn't know her name. Sandra and I, you know the new legal assistant, we call the bimbo the doorknob" I snort.

Liz looks amused. "What in the hell does that mean?"

I smile.

"Everybody has had a turn."

This time, we both burst out in a laugh.

Perking up, Liz asks, "Speaking of having a turn, what's the deal with you and Blaze?"

"No deal, just …" I try to decide if I should tell her what it is. *It's the best damn sex and I could be falling in —no, I'm not falling in love. It's his huge cock that I'm falling in love with.*

"Then what is it?" I hear the curiosity in her voice swinging in full effect.

I start to answer but close my mouth when I notice Hunter and Trey approaching us. They stand at the end of our table. I do my best to keep my eyesight on Liz, afraid to look at Hunter.

"Rose."

Hunter says my name as if nothing happened like he didn't call me a whore and pay for me to give him a lap dance.

Looking at Liz, I reply to him, "You need to leave."

"Not without apologizing," Hunter says softly.

Trey snorts. Then walks over to an empty table. He calls the waitress over to order something.

I guess they are staying for a while.

"I'm going to the girl's room. I'll be back." Liz gets up and walks off, leaving me scared out of my mind to be alone with Hunter.

When he sits, I don't speak. I just look at him with a blank expression.

Hunter's face is swollen with large bruises around each eye and a busted lip. There's white tape across his nose, leaving me with the impression it's broken.

"Please leave," I mutter.

"Let me speak, and then if you want me to leave, I will."

My hands are shaking so badly. I place them on the table, trying to control them. Playing with my napkin helps the shaking.

Hunter reaches across the table to take ahold of them, but I quickly retrieve them, placing them in my lap.

Letting out a frustrating gust of air, he pulls his hands back.

"Rose, I was completely out of line at Red. When I saw you there … in that outfit, I lost it. I was wasted and wasn't thinking straight. I know I fucked up … can you forgive me?"

"Hunter, I …"

He lowers his head.

"I don't think this is meant to be," I say softly.

Whispering, he pleads, "Please, Rose. That was the only time and the last time I saw her."

His left eye twitches.

He's lying. His eye twitches when he lies. I don't think he realizes he has that habit. It gives me a new purpose to let him know what we had is over.

"No. Hunter, it's over."

Darkness flashes in his eyes. He stretches his arms out. I flinch, scared that he's about to strike me, but instead, he grabs the edges of the table, pulling himself up, causing his chair to smash to the floor. He bends, leaning over me, and our faces are an inch apart.

"You're going to regret this, Bitch!" He spits out his words with pure hatred. "You're nothing but a dirty whore. You wouldn't put out to me, but you're sleeping with those filthy men at that club."

He stands to his full height and yells out to Trey. They leave the restaurant, pushing the door open with force. Scanning my surroundings, I see everyone looking at me. Embarrassment fills me.

Liz picks up the chair and sits down, looking at me with pity.

God, when did my life become a soap opera?

"Do you want to talk about it?"

"Not really. I would rather go do some day drinking."

Liz smiles. "That can be arranged. Want to come over to my place? I can make some mixed drinks, and we can get slammed."

I smile at her. "Sounds like a plan."

***

I'm so tipsy, and the ringing in my head won't stop. We're lying in Liz's living room, drinking the last bottle of wine.

Closing my eyes, I throw my arm over, groaning, "Make the ringing stop!"

Liz laughs, "It's your phone!"

My vision is a little blurry, but I can make out the name—Blaze. *Ugh, I can't deal with any man right now, especially one that is so damn intoxicating.*

I send the call to voice mail.

When banging occurs at the door, Liz stumbles to the door. I know right away who it is. His voice is loud, causing a wave of want to run through my veins.

"What the hell, Rose?" Blaze booms.

I'm lying on the floor, looking up at Blaze standing over me. Another shadow appears, and I see Mark. His hungry eyes take in what Liz is wearing.

I don't know how, but we ended up wearing just our underclothes. I laugh—what at—no idea. I blame it on the wine.

"Well, if it isn't Mr. Cocky Pants." I laugh out loud again.

His nostrils flare as his chest rises.

I take in his oversize body with lean muscles that are outlined in his undersized shirt. I spot the growing bulge in his pants, and I feel heat flood my body. The pulse between my legs is quickly making me squirm on the floor. With a smooth, swift motion, Blaze scoops me up and asks Liz where the bathroom is.

I hear the click of the lock, then feel the cold countertop on my ass. His lips run along my neck as his tongue darts out, licking my sensitive spot. God, this man has complete control over me.

When he licks his way up to my ear, his voice is raspy. "Stay silent, or I'll punish you."

His hand rushes to my sex, as if he couldn't wait to feel me. Sliding my panties to the side, he pushes two fingers into me. I try to spread my legs a little more to accommodate him.

"This sweet pussy is mine—mine to eat, to fuck, to punish."

His pace picks up. He's hitting that spot—the spot that makes me scream out his name, only I can't scream. I start to buck. I want to come. Blaze pulls me to the edge of the countertop. Unzipping his jeans, he lines himself up and plunges into me with force. He grabs me under my thighs, lifting me and slamming me back down on his erection.

Oh God, it's so good.

His large cock is stretching me, building a strong orgasm. I bury my head into his neck. Biting down, I scream out my release. He backs me up to the wall, pushing his cock into me to the hilt. I feel his release as his cock throbs inside of me.

Both of us sweating, breathless, and sated, we stare into each other's eyes.

When he pulls out, I slide down the wall, feeling his ownership drain onto my inner thighs.

Feeling embarrassed about having sex in Liz's bathroom, I whisper, "I can't go out there after we just fucked."

Blaze looks at me with something swirling in his eyes. "We're more than fucking buddies."

"You're a player you don't date. I know what this is." I regret my words as soon as they leave my mouth.

He reaches into my hair, pulling me to him. "I don't give a damn about anyone else. Your pussy is all I think about. It's mine; you're mine. Don't forget it." Those sapphire eyes bore into me. "I'm not one of those little boys you're used to. I always take what I want, and it's you I want."

Butterflies fill my stomach at his words. I want to believe him, but they're just words. I don't want to be that same stupid girl who keeps making mistakes in believing the wrong men.

Swallowing, I speak with a shaky voice. "Let's just
___"

His lips crash into mine while his hands grab my ass.
I'm so fucked!

12

Blaze

It's morning. *Mo Rós darling* is lying in my bed. I kiss her temple as I head out. I am on my way to meet the Anderson twins. They called and said they had Bonnie's boyfriend.

I pull up at Red and park next to Mark's vehicle. He gets out of the car, meeting me at the entrance.

"Hey." Mark greets me.

I nod.

Opening the door, I hear the guys laughing. We walk into the bar area where they are pouring whiskey.

"Where's he at?" I just want to get this done. I need to be balls deep buried in Rose right now.

Crew, one of the Anderson twins, answers, "We have Bonnie's boyfriend in the basement. He says he didn't kill her and doesn't know who did. I say he's a lying toerag."

Crew slams back the shot of whiskey.

I take a deep breath. "Fuck, pass me a glass."

Crew fills the glass with whiskey, and passes it to me.

I drink it in one swallow then slam the glass down, I point to it needing another drink.

"Where did you find him?"

Crew takes another drink. "He was hiding out at his brother's house in Portland." Crew shakes his head. "I can't imagine why he was hiding there. The dumb fucker had to know we would look there first."

I toss the drink back. Raising from the barstool, I walk toward the basement. The others follow me.

When I come around the corner, I hear Bonnie's boyfriend sniffle. I roll my eyes. Bonnie always did pick the biggest pussies to fuck.

I grab a seat and pull it up to sit down in front of him.

My voice is low and laced with poison. "I'm only giving you one chance. Don't fuck it up."

I'm not in the mood for this shit. I want to get home to Rose before she gets up. I know her tight arse will be trying to get out of my penthouse, only she will find that she has been locked in.

My reputation has its downfalls. One of them is Rose finding out my player ways, which made her doubt that I would be falling for a girl of her nature. She's a good girl with a strong head, but it won't change the way I feel for her. I'm determined to make her mine.

Pulling my attention back to the fucker in front of me, I reach out to pull his head up. He flinches, making his chair fall back.

Christ's sake. I haven't even touched the fucker.

I motion for Drew—Crew's twin, to pick him up. We're all arses, but the Anderson twins are in their own league. Drew picks him up by his hair, pulling a chunk out.

"As I said, you're only getting one chance. I'll know if you're lying. Be careful and don't fuck with me, or I'll put a bullet in your head."

The stupid fuck nods.

"When was the last time you saw Bonnie?"

He wipes his nose on his shoulder before answering, "We broke up a month ago."

That takes me a little off guard. I thought they were still together.

"Why?"

He looks at his feet. Following his eyesight, I notice he doesn't have shoes on. For fuck's sake, it's one of the weirdest quirks of the twins. They always take off the shoes of whomever they are torturing. They keep shoes as mementoes.

He lets out a sob. "She was fucking someone else."

Of course she was. A girl like Bonnie, from a fucked up lifestyle, tried to whore herself around just to try and land a man with money.

"I think it was someone she was working with, but she wouldn't tell me. We got into a huge fight. I wanted more, and when I told her I loved her, she laughed at me.

Said she had someone that was coming into a large sum of money soon. And I left.”

My mind goes to Rose. What if she tries to sleep with someone else? I slam my fist into the dude's face. Blood squirts out, covering his face.

Fuck! I didn't mean to hit him. I lost my temper when I thought of Rose being with another man.

Just a few moments ago, Mark had a look of boredom. Now, he's smiling like he's won a Nobel Prize. He pushes off the brick wall, walks over, and bends down to the guy's face.

“I would have cut your fingers off one by one,” Mark sneers.

Mark is the worst of all of us. I think he truly gets enjoyment from dismembering bodies.

My cell rings.

“Wilder.”

“What have you found out?”

“Nothing of any use. We're just getting started.”

The guy starts bellowing like a baby.

“Shut him up,” I command.

Mark smiles and reaches for his knife.

Fuck! “Mark, we need him to talk.”

Mark looks disappointed. I know why. He was about to cut his tongue out.

Hanging up with Wilder, I get back to my interrogation.

“Tell me everything from the time Bonnie woke up till she came home. Tell me anything that changed over time before you broke up.”

***

It's been a few weeks since we interrogated the pussy in the basement. The only new information we have is that Bonnie was fucking someone else besides him. We're working on trying to find out who it was, but we still don't have any more information than we had before. Things have been really quiet around the club, just normal business as usual.

I told Rose to be ready for me to pick her up tonight. I'm taking her to my favorite spot in town. I've been trying my best to give her time without suffocating her, but I'm growing impatient. I'm not used to a woman not wanting to bounce on my dick.

I arrive at Rose's apartment building. Walking into the building, I see her exiting off the elevator. She's stunning, wearing a red fitted dress that clings to her curves. Her hair is down and brushing the sides of her face. My dick twitches.

I see the gentlemen standing in the corner of the lobby eyeing her. I give them death warnings with my glare. I need everyone to know this stunner is mine. Strutting up to her, I slide my arm around to her arse, squeezing a hand full. Fuck, it's perfection, completely made for me. I want to slip under that dress and lick her from front to back.

She blushes. "Not here," Rose states.

I don't give a shit who sees me. She's mine. "I was coming up to retrieve you."

"I didn't want you to have to come up. I can meet

you here." She looks around the lobby.

I shake my head. Taking a deep breath, I tell myself to stay calm.

Grabbing her hand, I lead her straight to my car. Opening the door for her, she slides in ever so seductively.

"Thank you." She smiles.

When we leave the apartment complex, Rose asks "Where are we going?"

"I'm taking you to one of my favorite places to eat." I pick up her hand, kissing the back of it.

"Where?"

"You'll see."

I see her out of the corner of my eye. She's smiling, looking out the window, taking in the city lights.

We walk into the dark restaurant. This mum-and-pop place has been here for years. It's one of the best places to eat at.

The waiter comes up to greet me. "Mr. Walsh, follow me."

"You know I never knew your last name until now," Rose remarks.

The waiter motions for Rose to sit across from me.

I take her hand. "She'll sit beside me. Give us a few minutes to look over the menu," I instruct the waiter.

Rose sits in the booth, concentrating on the menu. I rest my hand on her thigh, pushing her skirt up.

"What are you doing?" she whispers.

I growl, "What I want to eat isn't on the menu."

Her eyes find mine. I run my fingers over her panties.

The waiter returns, asking us if we're ready to order. I don't move my hand. I casually view Rose's face.

She swallows. "I'll have …"

Pushing her panties to the side, I push my finger into her. Rose's eyes flutter, and she does her best to place her order. Pushing another finger into her wetness, I slowly move them in and out of her. I want her needy by the end of the night.

"For you sir?"

I look at Rose. Pulling my fingers out of her, I place them into my mouth, sucking them. "Mmm."

Rose stares at me in shock. Her cheeks are the prettiest shade of pink.

"The regular," I say to the waiter.

I've been here thousands of times. They know what I order. It's the same every time I come. One could say I'm a creature of habit.

Once the waiter leaves, I place my hand on the back of Rose's neck, pull her close, and kiss her lips softly. They're my favorite part of her. Her lips are soft and plump, and they look completely perfect around my cock.

The night moves along quite well. Rose seems to enjoy herself. She's not once, pushed me away.

My phone rings, breaking our conservation.

"Yes?" I look up at the ceiling. "Hmm … I see …" I look over at Rose. "Fine, I'll see you in the a.m."

Hanging up the phone, I announce, "I have to go out of town for a bit. I'll be back as quickly as I can."

She looks down. "Oh, there's no need to explain yourself to me. We're …" She trails off.

"We're what, Rose?" I bark.

I can't seem to get it through to her that I want more from her than just pussy. This thing I feel for her is new to me. I've never felt this way about anyone, but I'm willing to explore what this really could be. Waiting for her reply, I do my best to be patience.

"Well, you know …"

I raise a brow. "No … I don't. Explain."

She nervously pushes her food around her plate. "I know your reputation and I don't expect—"

Grabbing her chin, I pull her face to look at me. *"Mo Rós darling, I—"*

My phone rings.

Fuck!

"I have to get this." I pick up the phone. It's Mark. I know it's not good. He's tracing someone in Chicago that owes the club big-time money. He's good at what he does, only he needs more help to trace the fucker down. I don't understand why high-society pricks think they are entitled to anything they want without paying.

Slamming the phone down, I throw some money on the table. "I have to leave now. We'll pick up this discussion when I get back."

13

Rose

It's been two weeks since I've heard from Blaze. He's not texted or called. I wonder who he's fucking now. I forcefully wipe down my table. It's not that I want a relationship, but just thinking he might be with someone else makes me want to kick him in the balls. Telling me I need to quit my job. I pop the towel, place it on the booth, and scrub the seats.

I'm so lost in thought, thinking about Blaze being with another woman, and I don't hear someone when they walk up behind me.

"Rose!" Brady yells.

"WHAT?" I scream.

"Sorry, I didn't mean to scream at you."

I exhale.

"I've been standing here, calling your name for five minutes. You must have been in deep thought. Everything okay?"

"Yeah, just thinking about school." I lie.

I'm not ready to tell anyone about Blaze. The last thing I want is for my co-workers to think I'm just like all the other girls he's been with. I want to be more. I want …

I wipe the thought from my mind.

"Do you need a ride tonight?" Brady smiles.

He really is good-looking.

"I have my car and car keys."

We laugh.

"I'd be happy to take you if your keys come up missing again!" He wiggles his eyebrows and heads to the VIP section.

I notice Pepper seating several men at one of my booths. Grabbing my pen and pad, I walk over. It's the same guys who were with Mr. Wallace. I start taking their orders when lips brush up my neck.

Someone whispers, "Hello … beautiful."

Mr. Wallace.

"Rose, you smell delicious."

I pull away, not wanting to be so close to him. He smells of whiskey and sex.

"Thank you."

"Get the fuck back from her!"

Thank God it's Brady.

Mr. Wallace steps back with his hands up, surrendering.

Brady looks at the group of guys, then back to me.

I know he's trying to decide if he needs to remove them.

"Brady, he's fine. I will call out for you if I need to."

He nods and gives the men at the booth a death stare. Mr. Wallace receives the longest glare.

"Rose," Mr. Wallace purrs.

Mr. Wallace's look-alike calls out to him, "Come on, John. Sit down."

Mr. Wallace frowns at his friend.

"I'm Jacob Wallace." He smiles, stretching his hand to me.

I shake it, my mind going to what he said his last name was. It makes sense for them to look so much like. They're brothers. Jacob is extremely good-looking. His hair is shaved short on the sides and a bit longer on the top. Reminding me of a military cut. He's big, like I picture someone who's in the military.

He introduces the other men as his brothers. They have similar features, but Jacob and John could passed as twins.

Jacob is able to get John to sit down. He's completely drunk off his ass.

When I finally get Mr. Wallace and his friends settled down, my shift ends. I'm leaving early today. I'm picking up my high school friend, Sarah. She recently lost her job and is staying with me for a week. I'm hoping she will move to New York. She needs a change in atmosphere.

Closing my locker, I wrap my bag under my arm, when the door swings open. Two girls walk in, talking. I can tell by one of their voices that it's Pepper. They're talking about Blaze. This piques my interest. I back up in a corner, where I'm out of sight.

"We look really good together. It's just a matter of time before he's trying to crawl back into my bed." Pepper giggles.

"Well, I get the feeling he's interested in Rose. Do you see the way he looks at her?"

Pepper coughs. "No fucking way. She's such a prude. There's no way he'd be interested in someone like her."

They emerge out of the bathroom stalls.

"I'm just saying, I've been here a long time, and I've never seen him look at anyone the way he looks at her."

Pepper chokes out, "He looks at everyone that way until he sleeps with them. He's just a playboy with a big toy."

They both laugh.

I hate that he's been with so many women. I thought that maybe I could just sleep with him, and that would be it, no feelings, but I can already feel something forming inside of me, and it hurts, thinking about him being with someone else. I know exactly what I need to do to get over this feeling for him.

***

I'm so excited! I've called my good friends, hoping to meet up with them at Club Z. I've gotten Sarah up, and now, we're getting dressed to head out.

After we pay the cab driver, I spot Liz and Vinnie in

line. I scream out in excitement, running to them. I haven't been out in so long.

I push all thoughts for Blaze out of my mind. I'm hell-bent on having a good time tonight. I'm going to dance and flirt with every eligible, good-looking bachelor. Fuck Blaze and his huge dick. If he can't even pick up the phone to call me, then screw him.

We walk into the club and head for the bar. Once the bartender makes our drinks, we spot a free table. All four of us sit, talking and laughing. I'm enjoying hanging out with my friends. It feels like forever since we have been able to spend time like this.

Sarah and Vinnie head off to the dance floor while Liz is typing out a text. I start scanning the room to find someone to dance with. When I feel something cold against my arm, I go to embrace myself against the cold chill. But I accidentally knock over a glass tumbler. Looking down at the broken glass, I hear a deep voice speak.

"That was my fault. I shouldn't have startled you like that." A familiar face smiles back at me. It's Jacob Wallace.

Standing in shock, I open my mouth and then close it. My God, this man is simply breathless. He's dressed in a dark pair of jeans and a white dress shirt with his sleeves rolled up. His skin is golden and looks like it's been kissed by the sun.

The waitress comes over to clean up the broken glass and spilled drink.

"Would you like to dance?" Jacob stretches his hand out.

Eager to dance, I nod, placing my hand in his. I don't get the same feeling as I do with Blaze. Blaze's touch sends electric volts through my whole body.

Jacob has me laughing and dancing for what seems like hours. I'm out of breath. He's been going non-stop, and something tells me he could go non-stop at other things too. The man knows how to move. Finally, I tell him that I need a bathroom break.

I head down the dark hallway, trying to steady myself. My feet hurt, and my legs feel like jelly. I hear footsteps, and then I get shoved into a dark space up against a wall. A loud sound occurs, resembling a door slamming shut; I try to scream, but a hand placed over my mouth muffles it. I hear a low rumble, and I freeze. I smell him. His scent fills my nostrils.

"Looks like you need another lesson in not letting anyone touch what's mine," Blaze snarls.

He removes his hand from my mouth. Turning me to the wall, he places my hands on it. My heart is racing. I'm confused, trying to think of the right words to say because how can I be his if he hasn't bother to contact me for two weeks?

"Stop," I say the word, but it's barely audible. "Stop. Don't."

He doesn't say anything. I feel the pull of my skirt as it rises over my hips. His hand slides down to my sex. His lips place kisses along my neck, and then he bites me. It's gentle at first, but then he begins to bite harder.

"Tell me, *Mo Rós darling,*"—he traces my sex, then moves to my ass, placing his thumb over my back hole

—. "Did you enjoy it as much as I did, here?"

My breath hitches when he pushes his thumb in. I squeeze my eyes shut. I've never thought, I would have enjoyed being touched there, but Blaze makes it feel so good. It feels dirty and erotic all at the same time.

"Answer me." He demands.

I nob.

He pushes his thumb in. "Words Rose."

My voice is hoarse, but I manage to whisper, "Yes."

I can feel his smile against my neck as he places small bites, leaving goose bumps when he draws back.

I hear him unbuckling his belt, then the sound of his zipper becoming undone. My breathing becomes heavy when I feel him nudge himself at my back entrance.

"Bend over and touch your knees." His hand slides up my spine, bending me down.

"This will be your punishment for not listening. You're not to come, or I'll punish you with my belt."

His cock thrusts into my sex. Each thrust becomes harder while he flicks my clit. I'm a wet, panting mess. The building of needing to come is too much, too great to hold back. When he pulls out of me, I immediately feel the loss of him, but then I feel him. He's slowly pushing himself into my back entrance.

I tense. "Wait."

"You're going to learn that, I don't share."

Then, he's inside of me. Tears trickle down my cheeks, making their way to drip off my chin.

He lets out a moan of pleasure. "Oh fuck!"

His hand reaches down to my clit, massaging it. As

he starts to slowly move, I relax, starting to enjoy the feel of him. The pressure of him rubbing my clit and his cock in my ass cause a stronger buildup of an orgasm. He's picking up the pace of his thrusts and it coincides with the rubbing of my clit.

The building of an orgasm is great I want to come, I want to beg him, but my pride won't allow it. When he pounds into me one more time, he pulls my hips to him, burying himself completely releasing his seed.

When he pulls out, it burns. I feel his cum gush out and slide down my inner thighs. I pick up my clutch. Fumbling around, I get a tissue to clean myself.

"No." His voice is sharp. "I want my scent on you."

"Blaze, I'm not walking around, smelling like sex," I whisper-yell.

He leans into me, but I stand tall. I won't be walking around, smelling of sex.

"You'll do as I tell you, or I'll make your new friend … disappear."

"Seriously, what is wrong with you?"

"I told you … I want you, all of you, and I won't stop. You're mine. Now, let me help you get dressed."

His words send a shiver straight to my sex.

"No, don't touch me." I can't trust myself right now. I want to give him more of me, but am I willing to have my heart broken again?

The darkness is preventing the sight of his beautiful face, but I know he's not happy by the growl that escape his lips.

Once I'm finished getting myself together, we walk

out of the closet.

He's walking at my side with his hand resting on my lower back.

"Where are you going?" I question him.

His eyebrow lifts. "To make sure you do as I tell you. Not to let another man touch you."

"No, you're not. I don't want anyone to know what is going on between us." I smile. "You're my dirty little whore." With a smirk on my face. I walk away, leaving him.

14

Blaze

I'm her dirty whore? What the fuck? I shake my head, watching her arse. I'm still standing here like a damn puppy dog. I'm no one's dirty whore. It's always been the other way around, but not with Rose. I hate that she has me imprisoned. I don't want her as my dirty whore. I want her.   She leaves me to go back to her friends. Darting around, she tries to lose me in the crowd. Does she really think she could shake me off? Fuck no. I let her think she can, but I have eyes on her.

I spotted her when I walked in the door at Club Z, dancing with some fucker. He's lucky she was walking off, or he would have lost a hand.

Taking an interest in watching her has become my

favorite hobby. She has something about her that I'm completely transfixed on. Her beauty outshines everyone surrounding her.

My trip to Chicago was a mess. We finally traced down the fucker, and only got half of the money he owed to us. The other half was taken when he took the last air out of his lungs.

I need to go upstairs. The reason for coming here tonight was to meet a potential client, a business associate for Red. This could help establish more clients along the coast, possibly opening another club like Red. I just so happened to spot Rose.

Walking into the glass enclosed room, I see Wilder and Mark are already seated at the head of the table. Once I take a seat on the leather sofa, I stretch my legs.

When something slaps my shoulder, it startles me.

Wilder stands in front of me, "Did you even hear anything that was being said?"

"What?" I look around. The room is empty now. "Where the hell is everyone?"

Wilder laughs. "Man, you've got a bad dose."

"Fuck off!" I stand up and walk out.

The fucker is still laughing.

Fuck! I didn't even know I'd drifted off. I have got to get my shit together. This woman is going to be the end of me, if, I don't get her in check.

I spot Rose and her friends on the floor below. I watch them, making sure Rose doesn't dance with that fucker or anyone else.

I'm standing on the balcony when Mark comes up

beside me. He's looking in the same direction I am, but I have a feeling he's looking at a different woman than me.

"Wilder wants you to get some information on Rose's friend," he says while he keeps his eyes glued to something.

"Who?" I question him.

"That pretty strawberry-blonde that's sitting with Rose."

I haven't even noticed anyone besides Rose. I glance at the others at her table. Not liking what I see.

Fucking Vinnie.

"What's the interest?" I ask Mark.

"Seems to be liking what he sees." Mark turns toward me. "You know how women can be. Grab you by the balls and lead you around. If … you're not careful." He grins. "Just pull information on her, everything, then give it to him. She's staying with Rose—I know that." Mark slaps me on the shoulder and then walks off.

Fuck. Rose. Just thinking about her tight arse has my dick straining to be released. This new feeling is driving me insane. I've never felt so strong or had any feelings at all for any woman. I run my hands down my face, blowing out a breath. Shit, I'm screwed.

***

I sit at my desk, watching over everyone at Red. Rose is headed back home today from visiting her friend at Kitty Hawk. I inhale a breath of air, dreaming of being between Rose's legs, when Wilder walks in.

"Knew you would be up here," Wilder smirks.

I glare at him. I'm not in the mood. I haven't had my dick in Rose in over a week. Tonight, I plan on worshipping her body.

He laughs.

The fucker.

Taking a seat across my dresk, Wilder asks, "Any news on that fucker … Benny that showed his arse in the club?"

"We're working on it."

He nods. "Any new information on who Bonnie was sleeping with?"

"No. We had a lead, but when we got to the apartment he supposedly staying at, it was empty. Not even leaving a crumb for us to track. We'll get him, and when we do, I plan on letting Mark cut his legs off."

Wilder doesn't even flinch. He's used to hearing about the ruthless details of Mark's victims. Mark is dark. Darker than me or Wilder together. I don't know his full story, but I can only imagine it has to be disturbing.

"Do you want to have a drink?" Wilder stands, motioning to the whiskey I have in my office.

"I'm headed out in a few. I wanted to make sure Brady was doing his job. The fucker has the attention span of a two-year-old. Too busy chasing pussy."

Wilder lifts an eyebrow. "Remind you of anyone?" He tilts his head. "Keep me updated on what's going on. I want a piece of the fucker who thought they could come in our club and pull some shit like that and get away with it." He walks out.

I put my focus back on the camera noticing Brady has left the floor—again. Mother fucker, this kid needs to be let go.

I slide my phone into my pocket, grab my keys, and head out. I need to find that kid and teach him a lesson. He needs to stay focus and keep his eyes on the girls and clients.

I've looked in all the dark corners to try to find that motherfucker. He's nowhere in sight. There's only one place I haven't looked. I stare at the door that leads into the ladies locker room, wondering if Brady's arse is in there.

I walk up to the door, easing it open. I hear giggles, then sounds of a woman sucking dick. A man's moaning is coming from one of the stalls.

For fuck's sake!

I shove the door open with force. My heavy footsteps lead me to the last stall. Pushing the stall open, I catch Brady with his pants down to his ankles, and his dick is in Pepper's mouth. Pepper looks up at me and smiles around Brady's dick. Brady doesn't have the same reaction. He's more on the *scared shitless* end of the stick, and he should be.

"After you put your dick back in your pants, get your arse up to my office," I bellow out.

I look back at Pepper, who hasn't even bothered to take Brady's dick out.

Stupid girl.

Storming back to my office, I run into Mark coming out of one of the rooms.

"What the fuck are you doing down here?" I ask.

"Fuck off. What's your problem?"

I huff. "Is everyone fucking on the job?"

"Blaze, get some pussy. You're cranky as hell."

He's right. I need some pussy, but there's only one pussy that gets my dick hard. I take a deep breath of air.

"Yeah, I just caught Brady getting his dick sucked off by Pepper. Fucking dosser."

Mark throws his head back, laughing.

"When I opened the door, Pepper didn't even bother pulling his dick out of her mouth."

"You know Pepper. She's always down for a good time. I think we both know that. Don't get mad at the lad. You two have a lot in common."

"What the hell is that supposed to mean?"

He raises an eyebrow. "Don't tell me you haven't fucked your share of women at work. I know you better."

Yeah, he's right I used to, but Rose is the only woman I want to fuck, the only one I'm interested in.

"I'm headed upstairs. I need to get to my office. Brady is waiting on me," I tell Mark.

"I'll head with you," Mark comments.

When we get upstairs, my office door is open, and Brady is sitting across from my desk. I walk in with Mark behind me. I take a seat at my desk, and Mark stands, looking out the window to the floor below. Wilder and I both have the best offices. We can see everything below, but I still like to watch the cameras. It gives me a better view of the transactions taking place.

"Brady, I should fire you for the shit you just pulled. Then again, I could let Mark cut your dick off."

Mark reaches into his pocket and pulls out his favorite switchblade. His face lights up. Brady's face goes pale. I get up and walk over to the edge of my desk, close to Brady.

"Tell me, Brady, did you fuck Bonnie?"

He swallows. His eyes move over to Mark.

I raise my eyebrows, waiting on his answer. This will determine if he gets to live.

"Yeah … yeah, just once or twice. She … she had a boyfriend and didn't want to ruin anything between them."

I look over to Mark. We know that Bonnie was fucking someone else besides her ex. Also, the killing had to be an inside job because the cameras were interfered with.

I lean in close. "Once or twice, huh?"

Mark walks closer to Brady.

Brady looks like he wants to run but doesn't. He knows better. He doesn't want to make that mistake because we'll catch him and it won't be pretty.

"Tell us … Brady, did you get tired of her? Was she cramping your style?" Leaning my body down over him, I say with a deadly tone, "How about I cramp your style?"

15

Rose

I set the heavy luggage down in my living room. I'm jet-lagged, and it's too quiet now that Sarah is gone. Needing to be around someone, I call Liz, but she doesn't answer, so I call Vinnie.

Right away, he answers with a chipper voice. "Hey!"

"Hey yourself. What's got you in such a good mood?" I smile into the phone. Vinnie is good-looking, but there's nothing there. We're more like siblings.

"Nothing. Can I not be happy that one of my best friends called me?"

I laugh. "Do you want to come over to hang out? We can order a pizza? My treat." I do my best to entice him.

"Food? Yep, I'm on my way," Vinnie says in an excited tone.

Twenty minutes later my doorbell rings. When I pull open the door, no one is there. I peer out, looking down the hall both ways. I notice there's an envelope attached to my door. I grab it. The elevator doors open, and Vinnie steps out. His face lights up, and I can't help but smile back at my friend.

"Where's the food?" Vinnie asks when he walks past me and straight into my apartment. I walk in behind him, shut the door, and lay the envelope down on the bar.

"I was waiting till you got here before I ordered."

Vinnie throws himself down on my couch.

I already know his favorite pizza. I place the call while we decide on a movie to watch. It's nice to have someone to share my space with. I enjoy my time to myself, but having someone here is nice.

***

The lights are off, the television is going, and the empty pizza box lies on the coffee table. Vinnie is stretched out on the couch, and I'm on the lounge chair when the doorbell rings. I keep my eyes glued to the screen as the movie plays, backing myself up to the door to open it. When I turn to see who it is, I almost jump out of my skin.

Jacob Wallace stands in my hallway, looking like every girl's fantasy.

"Jacob."

"Rose." He cocks a grin. "I hope, I'm not bothering

you. I didn't get the chance to get your information so John gave it to me."

What the ever-living fuck!

Blaze will freaking come apart if he sees him. I have to get rid of him ASAP.

"I'm watching a movie with a … boyfriend." No need to tell him we are just friends. He can think what he wants.

Vinnie places his hand on the door, pulling it a little farther open. He's not a small guy. Vinnie has a large frame. I wouldn't count him out on any fight.

"Can I help you?" Vinnie says in a deep voice.

Mr. Wallace doesn't look intimidated. "No, this is between Rose and me."

They stare at each other in a standoff. Someone clears their throat, and I instantly freeze. Ice runs through my veins.

"Problem, boys?"

Blaze grabs my hand, tucking me into him. My body fits perfectly into his. The radiating heat flowing from his body penetrates me to my core. He's holding me ever-so tenderly, not at all aggressive.

Jacob's eyes flare up with anger. "No problem at all."

Blaze is big. Larger than Jacob and Vinnie.

I'm guessing Jacob doesn't want to test the water with Blaze. He gives me a nod and walks toward the door for the staircase.

I look up and see Blaze staring down at me with affection in his eyes. That look—the look I have been longing for someone to look at me with—it's strange to be coming from him.

"Rose, I'm going to head out," I faintly hear Vinnie say.

I'm so lost in a set of sapphire eyes. "Would you like to come in?"

Blaze doesn't answer, he just leads me in, shuts the door, and leans down, kissing me softly on the lips.

When he cups my face, I notice the fresh cuts on his hands. Pulling his hands back, I ask, "What happened to your hands?"

"Nothing." He kisses me again. "I've thought about being inside of you all week."

I smile. "I've thought about you being inside of me."

***

After all the lovemaking and fucking hard, like our bodies needed each other to survive, we lie in the dark with a hint of light shining from the moon. Blaze has his head on my breast, caressing the other one. This is different from our normal. Tonight, Blaze has been tender, warm, and perfect in every move he has made. This side of him, I could find myself falling in love with him—completely and utterly. I keep reminding myself I'm not ready, not ready for the heartbreak that awaits me around the corner.

"What's going on in that head of yours?" Blaze asks.

"Nothing," I lie. I don't want to tell him of my fear of falling for him.

"Rose." He cups my cheek. *"Mo Rós darling,* tell me. I want you, all of you. I want to know of your thoughts, fears, and dreams."

He rises above me, sliding in between my legs.

We gaze into each other's eyes. I'm in awe of the passion his eyes hold. An emotion that I've never seen before. I know at this moment, I want to give this a chance —whatever this is.

"Mo Rós darling."

He glides himself into me. My body already anticipating his girth. I wench. I'm already sore from all the sex we've had tonight.

When our bodies are skin to skin, he pulls back slowly, and with a quick thrust, he slams into me.

"Tell me," he demands, slamming into me again.

My back arches, and I let out a cry. He's punishing me, drawing back slowly, and hitting me so hard. I need him to pick up the pace, but he takes it slow. Tormenting me.

"Nothing," I say between a yell and a cry.

"Liar," he yells. "Tell me or I'll punish that sweet arse of yours. It'll be with my belt, not my cock." He slams into me hard again; I feel the air leave me.

"Tell me you want me." He's losing control as he takes me harder. "Say it. You only want my cock —forever. You want me; you want to have my children."

What? My brain misfires.

My orgasm hits me like a freight train, blinding me with sparks. This incredible pleasure sends my body into small convulsions. I keep my eyes on Blaze. I see his eyes roll back as his orgasm waves through his body. When his eyes return to mine, I see the tenderness they held before he lost control. I don't want to break him. I don't want to be the one that breaks … us.

"Can we … let's just do this on the down-low." I give him a small smile. "I just don't want to jump into anything."

"I won't stand aside and let you be with anyone else." Blaze's anger emerges.

There he is. There's the Blaze that I know.

"I'm not saying we date others. I just don't want a serious relationship right now. I'm too busy working and trying to get finished with school. I don't want anyone at Red to know what is going on between us." That last part of my request is due to the fact that he's a big player. If this goes south, I don't want to be another woman at Red who has sucked him off.

"I'll agree … for a while, but if I see you ever trying to give anyone a lap dance again, I'll kill them." His eyes hold the dangerous words he spits out.

I swallow. I have no doubt he would. I nod, agreeing to his terms. He pulls me into him, wrapping himself around me. The feeling of his warm body relaxes me into a deep trance. I'm on the verge of falling to sleep when I hear the faint words Blaze whispers into my ear.

***

The next morning, I wake up. Sliding myself out of Blaze's tight grip, I tip-toe into the shower. I want to grab breakfast since there's nothing in the cupboards. When I finish up in the bathroom, I walk into the bedroom. Blaze is sitting up with the sheet draped across his lap. He looks so edible with muscles showcased, golden-kissed skin, and tattoo's that emphasize the badass he is. He gives me a cocky grin, the arrogant bastard. I already know what he's up to.

"Blaze don't."

He throws the sheet back and his beautiful hard, thick, cock springs up at me. Literally points to me, like it's directing me to come to it.

Blaze smiles, and I know to run. I start to run to the bedroom door, but when I get picked up, I squeal out. He throws me onto the bed and pins me down.

I giggle loving this playful side of him. "Let me go." I wiggle under him. "I was going to surprise you with a large breakfast."

He says, "Hmm," while placing kisses on my neck. "What I want to eat is right here." He cups my sex.

"That sounds … perfect, but I need food in my stomach." I'm not lying. I'm so hungry.

Last night's events have left me famished. I push him off, but he holds onto me rotating us so I'm sitting on top of him.

"Suck my cock. If you're a good girl and swallow every drop, I'll take you out for breakfast."

I roll my eyes. Then, I do what he asked and swallow every drop.

***

I reach for my keys at my breakfast bar and notice the envelope I placed on the bar last night. When I pick it up, Blaze walks over, standing over my shoulder.

"What's that?"

"I don't know. It was on my door last night when Vinnie came over."

Blaze blows out a breath of disapproval at the mention of Vinnie's name.

I open the letter, and the words *revenge is mine* are printed in large bold letters. My hand shakes as I try to hold myself steady.

Blaze pulls the letter out of my hand. I'm trying to stay calm, but I almost jump out of my skin when my cell rings. Pulling it out of my purse, I take in a deep breath when I see it's my mother.

"Hello?"

'Rose, baby. Are you okay?" I hear the fear in my mom's voice.

"Yeah, I'm okay. What's wrong?"

"Oh, honey, your dad has been receiving threats for weeks. We didn't want to get you and Lilly involved, but now, the threats have been … mentioning you and Lilly. I'm so sorry. We were trying to protect you both. We have received the second threat that pertains to you both, and we're contacting the police. Lilly is on a plane to come home. Can you catch a flight home today?"

Blaze listens in on our conversation, shaking his head. I chew on my nails. An uneasy bubble rises from my stomach to a hard knot in my throat. Could this be in connection with the decline in my dad's business?

"Mom, don't worry. I'll be okay." I look up at Blaze who seems beyond angry. He gives off the appearance of bloody pissed off.

"Everything is going to be okay," I reassure her.

16

Blaze

Rose gets off the phone with her mother, and I see the color has drained from her face.

"Rose." I look down at the letter. My blood boils at someone threatening my girl. *My girl.* It's a strange feeling —to care about someone other than myself. It's been so long since I cared for anyone. My parents were the last ones that I felt the need to protect.

I cup Rose's face. She tilts her head, relaxing into my palm.

"Mo Rós darling, I'm going to protect you."

She looks up at me with tears welling in her eyes.

"Why don't we go grab that breakfast?" I say to her.

I want to get her mind off of this fucked up mess.

"Okay," she says but it's barely audible. I know she is trying to hold herself together.

I take Rose's hand and lead her out of her apartment and the building. When we get to my car that's parked right next to Rose's, we come to a standstill. Rose's car has been completely trashed. Windows busted, tires slashed, and graffiti written on every spec of the surface.

I pull Rose to me, burying her head into my chest. She lets out a sob. I'm not sure what the hell is going on but I intend on finding the son of a bitch who dared to fuck with my girl.

With one hand on Rose and the other reaching into my pocket for my phone, I call Mark.

"Mark, get your arse down to Rose's apartment. You got the address?"

He replies, *"Tá."*

I know he already has the address. We all have the addresses of everyone who works at Red. Keeping tabs on their home and where their family lives are very important. Everyone has to be checked out before we allow them to work for us. We don't want to let any of our enemies inside to fuck us over.

I speak into Rose's soft, dark hair. "You're going to stay at my place."

She looks at me with red eyes. "Blaze …" She looks at her shaking hands. Balling them up into fists to try and keep them from shaking, she says, "I need to be strong. I can't let whoever this is win. That's what they want. They want to break my family. Why, I don't know. We've never harmed anyone."

"Fine." I blow out air. "I'm staying with you."

She doesn't say a word. She accepts my presence in her apartment. Maybe she's more scared than she would like to admit. Whatever it is I'm thankful. She would not have won the battle over me staying with her. Mark pulls up and parks behind Rose's car. I pull Rose to my car and tell her to sit while I speak to Mark. Closing the passenger door of my car, I walk over to Mark. He's standing up against his car, shaking his head.

"Who has the balls to mess with your lady?" Mark asks.

"Someone looks to be getting desperate to have this reaction. Rose and her whole family have been targeted. Do you think there could be some kind of connection between Bonnie and this fucked up shit?"

Mark shrugs his shoulders. "Don't know, but I'll look into it." He pulls out a stick of gum.

"You having any luck, giving up cigarettes?" I raise an eyebrow.

He pops the stick of gum into his mouth. "As long as something is in my mouth, I'm fine." He grins.

I laugh. *Dirty bastard.*

"Get someone out here and take this off. It's still early, and I don't think anyone else is up."

He makes a call, and fifteen minutes later, Rose's car is being hauled off. I slide into the driver's seat of my car and start the engine.

"I need to fill out a police report."

"No, we have got it under control," I tell her.

"Blaze, I need to do this the legal way," she says

with a firm tone.

I stop the car and turn to her. *"Mo Rós darling,* whoever started this will pay. The outcome won't be in their favor. Be a good girl and just do as I ask. You're mine. I'm going to make sure the fucker who did this … pays."

***

It's been days and I'm never far away from Rose. I sit at the bar at Red while she works her tables. I feel the tension in Rose has eased up in the last day. I'm just hoping we don't have any more cluster fucks. My phone vibrates in my pocket. I see Mark's name pop up on the caller ID.

"Tá." I wait for him to reply.

"We got him. Coming through the back entrance, headed for the basement."

"Who?" I question him.

"The boy Bonnie was sleeping with."

"Be there in five." I hang up.

I know Rose wants me close by. I've noticed how she keeps looking over her shoulder to make sure I'm still here. So, I need to let her know that I need to step away.

When I walk up behind her, I place my hands on her hips. It startles her a bit. I lean down to her ear. The men in the booth look on with envy. I don't give two fucks.

"I have to step away. DO. NOT leave the floor for any reason."

She looks up at me with those beautiful doe eyes, and I take her lips with mine. Kissing her softly, I pull back, biting her bottom lip.

Fuck! She tastes so good.

I adjust my dick and walk off.

When I get down to the bottom of the basement stairs, I hear a cry for help. I roll my eyes.

Bonnie's fucked up taste in guys.

Coming around the corner, the fucker raises his head, and his eyes go wide. Good. He recognizes me. I also remember him.

What's this fuckers name?

"Are you acquainted with each other?" Mark asks.

I smirk. "Something like that."

I walk up and stand behind the fucker.

"What's your name boy?" I bark out.

"I'm not a boy, and it's Hunter," he says with irritation in his voice.

If he's intimidated, he doesn't show it. For some reason, his arrogance infuriates me.

"Hunter. That's right." I circle him, talking. "You remember me?"

He nods.

I give him a crooked grin. "Good … then you are well aware that I don't put up with bullshit." I keep circling him. "I have questions. I want answers. I know you have those answers."

Hunter slumps in the chair trying to relax.

I shake my head. Less than five minutes in the same room with him, and I already want to kill him. What the fuck was Rose thinking, dating a loser like this?

I look over to Mark. He has a dazed look on his face, and I know what he wants to do to make this boy

show some respect. I nod to him and down at Hunter.
Words don't have to be said.

Mark comes over, and we untie Hunter's hand from his back.

"What the fuck are you doing?" Hunter wiggles around, trying to get loose. The worry lines on his young face show he's finally decided to take us seriously.

Mark ties back his left hand while I pull the right hand out on the table, holding it there. Drew brings over a hammer. This hammer is the truth seeker. Very few men hold out on information when the truth seeker gets involved.

"No… don't. Okay, okay. I'll tell you whatever it is you want to know," Hunter begs.

I'm not letting him get off that easily. I'll hear him out, and then I plan on smashing the fucker's hand. I don't want him anywhere near Rose again. I need to make sure I get my point across to him.

I start questioning him. "Were you fucking Bonnie?"

Hunter nods.

"Words," I demand.

"Yeah. Yes, I was," he barks out.

Hunter answers a few more questions for us, and I know he's not the one who killed her.

I pull Mark to the side. "What led you to him?" I tilt my head toward Hunter.

"His bank account, for one. Bonnie's ex-boyfriend said the guy she was fucking was coming into a lot of money. His bank account has been receiving large amounts of deposits."

"Where are they coming from?" I look back over at

Hunter. Who's staring at us with anger on his face.

"We're working on tracing it. It's a little hard because it's coming from an offshore account."

Fuck.

I'd be lying if I said I didn't want it to be him. I just want to put a bullet in his head and dump him in the East River.

I slowly let out a breath of air. "Let's hold him till we can find out where he's getting the money and from who."

"Will do." He starts to walk off.

"Mark."

He turns to me.

"I didn't say we couldn't have a little fun." We both laugh.

Picking up the hammer, I stand in front of Hunter.

"Stay away from Rose. She's not yours, and if I see you around her again, I'll kill you," I puff out.

"Fine, she's damaged goods anyway. Anyone who sleeps with men for money is nothing but a dirty whore."

I can see Mark's anger rise along with my temper. How fucking dare he call my Rose a dirty whore.

Then, with a quick movement, I raise the hammer. The panic look of fear is clearly written on Hunter's face, but to my surprise, he doesn't beg. I slam the hammer down, crushing the bones in his hand and fingers. He screams out in agony. I hear another scream behind me. It's not a man's scream; it's a woman's. When I turn, Rose is standing with tears outlining her eyes as they make their escape down her pink cheeks. I never wanted her to see this side of me.

When I take a step toward her, she yells, "No …
don't you dare take another step."

I stand, looking at my love with my heart breaking
wide open.

"Rose," I whisper.

It's too late. She runs out of the basement.

17

Rose

I run as fast as my legs will allow. I make it out of the damp, dark basement that has the stench of blood lingering in the air. My mind is racing along with my heartbeat at the memory of witnessing Blaze smashing Hunter's hand. How could I fall for someone who could commit something so … brutal? Has he done worse? I'm so out of my mind with thoughts that I bump into someone.

"Sorry." I look up to see Brady smiling. "Brady, what happened to your face?"

"Oh … you mean, all the bruising I've got going for me?" he says lighthearted.

"Yeah, you look awful," I exclaim.

Brady still smiles, even after the non-compliment I gave him. He really is a great guy.

"I got the shit beat out of me."

Thinking back, I did notice Blaze's knuckles with scratches on them. "Did Blaze do that?"

He blows out air. "Yeah, don't take it the wrong way because he's just doing his job."

"Doing his job is not beating up every guy around," I scoff.

"Rose, being in this environment, you have to be tough. He has a huge responsibility. Don't be so rough on him. What he does, he does to protect, not the other way around."

I chew on his words. He's right. I should at least give Blaze a chance to explain.

"Why are you defending him when clearly, he messed up your face?"

He shrugs his shoulder. "I get it. It's a guy thing. Besides, do you know how many women are willing to do anything for a man with a couple of bruises?" He wiggles his eyebrows.

I laugh. Brady is truly adorable. I leave him and make my way to the locker room to gather my things.

I pull out my phone from my purse when I notice a couple of missed calls from Lilly.

The door bursts open, and Blaze storms into the women's locker room. Causing me to jump and drop my phone. I close my eyes praying, it didn't shatter. Peeking through hooded eyes, I see my phone is still in one piece.

Blaze storms over to me, staring at me intensely. My cell interrupts his glare. I pick it up and see it's Lilly. I throw up my hand at Blaze, motioning him to be quiet.

Answering my cell, I say, "Hey Lilly!"

"Lilly … is a bit … tied up at the moment," the male's voice breathes heavily into the phone.

"Who is this, and where's my sister?" I yell into the phone.

Blaze goes into high alert. My eyes fill with tears.

"You don't get to ask questions. You just do what I tell you to do, and you can see your sister again. Don't do what I tell you to do, and I'll cut her throat."

My hand covers my mouth.

Blaze asks, "Who is it?"

I wave him off. But he grabs the phone out of my hand.

"Who the fuck is this?" he bellows.

Blaze pulls the phone away from his face to view the caller ID. Putting his attention on me, he asks, "Who was that, and what did they want that got you so upset?"

I let out a sob and then fall to my knees. I'm so shaken. "Someone has Lilly. He threatened if I didn't do as he said, he would kill her."

I cry harder. Blaze might have just murdered my sister.

"Oh baby, I'm so sorry. I promise I'll find the motherfucker, and I'll see to it that he's punished."

Blaze pulls me up and wraps his arms around me.

"I need to call my parents. They need to know. Lilly was supposed to be on her way home to be with them."

Blaze dials my parents while I try to regain my composure. I need to be strong.

My mother's voice is so soothing when she answers

the phone. "Hello dear."

"Mom … Lilly—"

"She's right here. Do you want to talk to her?"

"What? She's there with you?"

"Yes, dear, I told you she was coming home. Here, Lilly … come get the phone. Your sister wants to speak to you."

It's a few seconds before she gets on the phone, and all I can think about is how my heart is racing away. The pain I felt from the call I received tore me in two.

"Hey, Rose!" Lilly says with excitement.

Lilly is truly a happy soul. So innocent and so different from the people I'm around on a daily basis.

"Lilly!" I almost can't believe she is there. "I'm so glad to hear your voice."

"Yeah, you too. You're acting weird. What's going on?" Lilly says with a wary voice.

I don't even pause. I dive straight into it. "Someone called from your phone and threatened that if I didn't do what they asked they were going to kill you. Where in the hell is your phone?"

"I lost it. I was in such a hurry to get home that I misplaced it. I can't believe someone did that."

"Maybe you didn't misplace it. Maybe someone saw the opportunity and took it when you weren't looking," I comment.

"Yeah, I guess. Everything got crazy at the airport. One minute, I had it in my hand, but I set it down and must have forgotten it."

"Think, Lilly. Was there anyone acting suspicious

around you at the airport? Did you notice anyone who was everywhere you were?"

She's quiet for a long pause. I wait on pins and needles, trying to be patient with her blindness to any activity that surrounds her. Lilly has always been that way. She doesn't pay as much attention to the things going on around her, and it worries me.

"No … I don't know. I don't recall anything."

She's hopeless.

"Okay, stay with Mother and Dad at all times. Tell them I love them, and for goodness' sake, start paying more attention to your surroundings. I'll call you and check in with you guys tomorrow."

After we say our good-byes, Blaze embraces me.

***

Blaze demanded I spend the night at his place tonight. So, we're wrapped up in each other in his plus-size bed. My head lies on his hard chest, and I tilt my face to look up at him.

"Why did you hurt Hunter?" I ask Blaze. I'm curious as to why he would smash his hand.

"He deserved it," Blaze says with a tight lip.

I prop myself up on my elbow. "I imagine Brady's face did something to deserve the beating you gave it?"

Blaze turns his beautiful blues to me. "Rose." He brushes the hair back from my face. "Sometimes, I have to do things that you won't understand, but know that I won't ever hurt you."

He rises and rubs his nose against mine. He presses his lips to mine, kissing me.

His lips are my ticket straight to hell. They're sinful. The way he works his lips, tongue, and cock is all too good.

I lightly push on his chest slightly presses him back to lie on the mattress while I climb on top of him.

Grinding and teasing his cock, "Tell me … what do you want from me?"

Blaze's eyes darken. He's looking at me so hard that I can feel them straight into my soul with heat. He's searching for something … feelings. My feelings for him.

"I want to give you what you want. What do you want, Rose?" Blaze says the words with sincerity in his voice.

I swallow. I'm finding it difficult to speak. To tell him, I want him and only want him to be mine. I know, I need to put my feelings in front so he knows where I stand.

"I want you to love me with your whole heart—forever—and I want you to fuck me like my body is the only body you will ever desire," I whisper.

Blaze sits up and I run my fingers through his hair while our lips lightly touch.

"*Mo Rós darling*, I've never felt this way about anyone. We're in this together."

His hands roam over my ass, squeezing it.

"This,"— his hands squeeze my ass a little harder —"I'm about to pound into."

He rolls us over and flips me onto my stomach. I giggle. I want it. I never thought I would enjoy getting taken in my back entrance. Somehow, it feels right with Blaze, but then again, a lot of things feel right with him.

Since I have been back from Kitty Hawk, it's been a whirlwind. I'm on a beautiful ride that I don't want to get off. Blaze has either stayed at my apartment or I have stayed at his. It's been pure bliss!

***

The next morning, Blaze says he wants to take me out to breakfast, but I don't have time. I'm in need of a shower from all the sex we had, and then I have to head to work.

I would have thought two jobs would make me tired. I seem to always get my second wind when I get off at Ross and Archer. I know Blaze is that reason.

Sarah should be making her way back to New York shortly. I'm looking forward to having her, but I'm hoping that this thing between Blaze and me will keep getting stronger. We seem to be on a slow steady way to having something unique between us.

We still have no idea who called from Lilly's phone. When we checked the GPS on the phone, it didn't display the location. We're guessing someone has busted the phone to keep it from being tracked down.

18

Rose

I sit down at my desk at Ross and Archer and start my morning routine. I've been really lucky thar Mr. Wallace has been out of the office since his last visit to Red. Sometimes, facing him is a bit much, especially after his special drink order. I mean, Death by Sex? Really?

Liz walks into the office, sunglasses cloaking her eyes.

Gathering my pen and paper, I walk over to her desk. I need to give the illusion of working in case a manager walks by.

I sit down in the chair beside her desk. "Hey."

Liz slumps in her chair. She accidentally knocks off a file. When she bends, down to pick it up, her glasses fall off.

I gasp, "Liz, what the hell happened to your face?"

She quickly picks her sunglasses up and puts them back on.

"I ran into a wall. I was too busy on my phone to see it," she says a little too quickly.

"Liz." I take her hand, giving it a squeeze. "You would tell me if something was wrong, right?" I try to read her, but she's got a wall up.

"Of course I would." She squeezes my hand back. "I really did walk into a wall … I think? I was looking down at my phone, reading a text, and the next thing I know, I was lying on the pavement." She exhales. "When I came to no one was in sight, and nothing was missing. I think I seriously just walked a little too hard into a wall."

I believe her. I've run into many walls. None of them have actually knocked me out, but it could happen.

"Are you going to tell me about you and Blaze?" Liz taunts.

I get a little excited, hearing Blaze's name. "You won't tell anyone, will you?"

"Mum's the word."

I feel the corners of my mouth move stretch across my face in a wide smile.

"We have been spending so much time together since I got back from Kitty Hawk, and I'm completely in heat over him."

"Rose, I've never seen you glow like this about anyone or anything."

"I know. It feels amazing. The sex is out of the world and it seems crazy but I think he has true feelings for me. He's just a little too overbearing at times but I can handle that." I laugh at the overbearing part.

It's true. I'm hard to handle at times, but I think we could balance each other.

"Just be careful. I've never known or heard of him being in any serious relationship." She holds her hands up in defeat. "I'm not saying he doesn't have feelings for you. I'm just letting you know what I think."

I know she's right, but I'm going with my heart.

"It's fine. Thank you for having my bad."

"You know I will always have my girl's back."

"Oh my gosh!" I say with excitement. "I almost forgot to tell you that Mr. Wallace—."

On cue, Mr. Wallace walks into the department, looking like a sinful slice of cheesecake. Every woman in the department stops what they're doing and stares him down. Walking beside him is his brother, Jacob.

Double the fun!

Jacob spots me and gives me a slow smile that would call to any girl's ovaries. I hear some of the ladies mummer under their breath with disgust. Jealousy really is ugly.

Liz whispers, "Who … is … that?"

Jacob touches his brother's shoulder, whispers something, and walks to us.

"Mr. Wallace's brother," I whisper as fast as I can before Jacob gets to us.

"Hello, ladies," Jacob says with a sexy, deep voice.

"Hi," Stevie says, bubbly.

Oh Lord! I cannot believe this heifer came over

here. She needs to get back on her broom and fly away.

Jacob barely turns his head when he speaks to say hello. I laugh a little on the inside. That's what you get when you come barging over without an invite.

Nosy bitch.

Stevie gets the hint and walks off. Mr. Wallace comes out of his office in a fury. He comes up to Jacob and practically drags him off. Doesn't even say a word, just grabs his brother's arm and pulls him to the elevator.

"What the hell was that about?" I ask no one. It's more of a statement.

Liz and I both watch on while it looks like Mr. Wallace gives the riot act. Seriously, they are in some heated conversation.

"Could you imagine having a threesome with them?" Liz comments.

"Are you serious?" I look at her—deadpan.

"Fuck yes." She smiles.

"I bet his brother is just as hung as he is." She puts her elbow on the desk, resting her hand under her chin. "I bet it would be cock heaven," she says in a dreamy state.

I roll my eyes. "Oh, I didn't get to finish what I was trying to tell you. So, anyway, Mr. Wallace came in—."

"What was he wearing? Tell me, were his pants tight and you could see the outline of his groin?"

"Yuck. Can you please get back to earth and out of cock heaven?" I scrunch up my nose.

"Liz, he leans over his table." I lean over to show her how seductive he was. "Then he dropped the bomb … I'll take Death by Sex."

Liz squeals.

"Keep it down." I shyly look around. "It was weird for him to order such a provocative drink, don't you think?"

"If he told me he wanted Death by Sex, I would have shoved him in the corner and made damn sure he felt like death after I got done."

I laugh my ass off.

***

It's late in the evening, and I'm headed to go get ready for Blaze to come over. I have decided to cook him his favorite meal—stew meat and potatoes.

I stop at the crosswalk and wait for my turn to go. When I get the green, I start to cross, but when I hear tires squeal, I look up to my left and have to jump out of the way because a black SUV comes right at me. Almost hitting me. My heart just fell in my shoes. I know that wasn't an accident. The driver was looking straight at me.

"Miss! Miss, are you okay?" A young man asks.

The young man helps me stand.

"Yeah, I'm fine." I stand, but my ankle gives me trouble.

I hop over to a bench to sit. Rubbing my ankle, I pull out my cell. I need to call Liz and see if she can pick me up. There's no way I can walk home. I walk to work because it's not that far from my apartment, and it gives me time to clear my mind.

"Hey, you miss me already?" Liz laughs.

"Liz, are you still at work?"

"I'm leaving now."

"I'm sitting on the bench in front of Bear's Bread. Can you please pick me up? I've twisted my ankle."

"Yeah, I'll be there in a few."

"Thank you."

Ten minutes later Liz pulls up and I hop into the passenger side of her car. When I buckle up, Liz speaks.

"What the hell happened to you?"

"Only that some asshole tried to run over me."

"Did they try to run over you, or did you walk out in front of them?" Liz says like she's afraid I might bite her head off.

"No, he tried to run over me. You know, he looked familiar. I didn't get a good look at him, but what I did see, I felt like I have seen him before."

We pull up to my apartment building, and I hop up to my apartment. Unlocking my door, I throw my purse and bag down. I pull my cell out of my pocket and call Blaze to see what time he's coming over. Hoping I can get him to come over faster.

"Mo Rós darling." Blaze purrs.

I swoon every time I hear him say those words.

There's a knock at my door.

"Blaze, hold on. Someone is at my door."

I hop up and over to the front door to open it. When the door swings open, Blaze is standing in the doorframe with dark jeans, a fitted green T-shirt, and a smile that makes my heart race.

I still have the phone to my ear, looking into those beautiful sapphires. "Hi," I breathe.

"Hi," Blaze whispers.

He comes in the door and slams it shut, backing me up into the apartment. He picks me up, and I wrap my legs around him until my ankle touches his back and causes me to wench.

"What's wrong?" Blaze questions.

"I fell and twisted my ankle."

I try to put my legs down, but Blaze walks us over to the couch, setting me down on it.

"Let me see."

Blaze runs his large hands along my ankle, which has swollen.

"I'll get you an ice pack."

Blaze goes into the kitchen, asking, "What happened?"

"I was crossing the street after work, and someone tried to run me over."

Blaze stops making the ice pack. He turns to me with a furious expression set on his face. For a moment, I wonder what I did.

"Someone tried to run you over?"

I nod.

"Did you get a look at them?"

"I got a glimpse. They had a baseball cap over their face, but something about their features looked familiar. I just can't place who it was."

"What were they driving?"

Blaze is hanging on by a string. I feel his anger building.

"Black SUV. I don't know what it was. I just know

it was black and it looked expensive.”

Blaze crushes the ice pack in his hand. His face is set in a daze.

“Blaze.”

He doesn’t answer. His face grows angrier.

I yell, “Blaze.”

He shakes his head, trying to pull his thoughts out of the darkness.

19

Blaze

My mind goes into a mass of flames when Rose tells me of her encounter with a dark SUV. One name comes to mind, someone who drives an expensive dark utility vehicle. Standing in Rose's kitchen, I pull my cell out of my pocket and dial the Anderson twins.

"Blaze," Drew yells.

There's loud music in the background, and then I hear a door slam, and it goes to complete silence. He must be at Club Z.

"Rose was almost hit today by a dark SUV. Tap into the street cameras and see if you can make out a tag. Also, give me Brady's whereabouts for today."

I give him the address of Rose's work, telling him to look at all the cameras in the surrounding blocks.

I know her normal routine from the tail I have on
her. What I can't figure out is why the hell my soldier didn't
tell me what happened to Rose.

Once I'm off the phone with the twins, I call Mark.

Mark answers without saying a word.

"Mark, I need you to get me that information
regarding Hunter's account now," I bellow.

"I should have it to you soon," Mark says.

He hangs up.

I need to keep calm. I don't want to scare Rose.
Somehow, I believe Bonnie's death and what's been
happening to Rose are tied together. I don't know how yet,
but I will find out.

I know that it wasn't Hunter who tried to run over
Rose because we still have that fucker tied up in the
basement. But Brady drives a dark truck, and I know he
has the day off.

I feel a tugging on my shoulder, causing me to come
out of my thoughts. Rose has a look of concern sketched
on her face.

"What is it, Rose?" I run my hand down her
delicate face.

She pulls up her cell and shows me a text with an
attachment of a photo from an unknown caller. It's Lilly, tied
up to a chair with duct tape around her mouth.

Large pools of water fill Rose's eyes. I take the
phone, looking at the picture closely. Rose falls into my
chest, gasping for air. There are no words I can say that
would make her feel better. I embrace her and do my best
to console her.

"Rose." I put my hand under her chin and pull her face up to look at me.

"I'm going to get this … person. I promise you, your sister will be okay."

I read the text the pussy sent. He tells her to come alone and gives her the address. I know the address, the whereabouts, and the location is not in a good part of town.

Rose tries to speak, but her crying is preventing her to get the full words out.

"Baby." I push her against my chest. "You're not going. It's not the side of town for a woman to be in."

She pushes against me. Gathering herself, she speaks, "I have to go. They only want me to come, and I have to go by myself."

I blow out steam that fills my lungs. I'm not in the mood to fucking fight.

"Rose!" I say too loud.

She shakes and starts crying again.

FUCK!

She's not in a state of mind to do anything. She can barely keep herself standing up.

I dial one of our soldiers—Zane, requesting him to come over to Rose's apartment, I call out Rose's address to him. I need to make sure she doesn't get out of the apartment. I know Rose is a strong-headed, woman and she will find a way to leave.

***

Twenty minutes later, Rose is lying in bed, and Zane

knocks on the door. Opening the door, I let him in. Telling him about what is going on and that I need him to keep guard till I can get back.

I call my soldiers, and we are meeting a block away from the house where Lilly is being held. Upon our arrival, we go over our plans for entering the house. I made a couple of drive-bys to check out the location of the house. How we can enter and see what vehicles were there. Lucky for us, there is only one vehicle, and I know it's fucking Brady's SUV.

"The house is an older home, a white 1930s country cottage. Mark, you will cover the back door, and I'll knock on the front while Drew and Crew will cover the sides. The house looks like a real shit-hole, so you guys be careful."

Mark smiles. He loves shit like this.

The Anderson twins smirk as well.

I shake my head, thinking of these guys and their fucked up ways.

I'm one lucky son of a bitch to have brothers like these men.

We head off, walking toward the house. We don't want to give any indication of our arrival, so we decided to park at the end of the block from the house and to walk the rest of the way so as not to alarm the fucker. Everyone gets in position. I ease my way onto the porch, looking through the small window on the front door. I hear noises coming from the house. Sounds of a woman screaming. I know it's now or never. Pulling my foot up, I kick the lock as hard as possible, and it busts the door down. I hear the same for the back door, and Mark and I run into the room where the screams are coming from. Guns drawn, we enter the room. More screams erupt upon our entrance. It's fucking Brady in bed with a woman on him naked.

"What the fuck?" Brady yells.

"Don't fucking move," I say with my gun pointed at him.

Mark rushes through the house, looking for Lilly.

Drew and Crew come into the bedroom, giving the woman a look over. Leave it to them to be having thoughts of fucking.

Mark comes back into the bedroom where we are all gathered around Brady and the young woman.

"All clear. There's no sign of Lilly anywhere." Mark tells me.

I point the gun at Brady's temple. "Where the fuck is she?"

"I don't know who the fuck you are talking about, man," Brady yells.

"Cut the shit. I know you tried to run over Rose, and now, you have Lilly tried up. So, where is she?"

Brady swears again that he doesn't know what I'm talking about. Mark pulls me to the side.

"Listen, there's nothing more I would rather do than fuck him up—you know that—but are we sure it's him? Someone is planning a dangerous game. Could it be that they are trying to set him up?"

I look over to the young lad. He's Irish, just like us. Just like us, he has no one. The only family he has is an uncle back in Ireland. His uncle is a client and a good friend of ours. Brady's uncle called me personally and asked me to give the lad a job. Wanted me to help him find his way. Brady has turned out to be a tougher case than I imagined.

I throw the girl her clothes and tell her to get dressed. When she makes herself disappear into the bathroom. I pull a chair up to the side of the bed. Taking a seat, I look hard at Brady.

"Where have you been today?" I question him.

"I've been right fucking here," Brady says with a tone I don't appreciate.

I prop my elbows on my knees. "If you use that tone again, I'll blow out your kneecaps. Doing them one by one. Do I make myself clear?"

Brady blows out air from his mouth and nods.

"Good." I sit back up and proceed. "Now, give me your whereabouts today."

Brady comments that he's been home most of the day, banging the chick he picked up at the coffee shop. When the girl comes out of the bathroom, I look her in the face. I've seen this girl before. She's a hooker. I tell her to sit.

I look at Brady. "You meet her at a coffee shop?" I snort.

"Yeah," Brady says with a short tone.

He doesn't seem pleased I find it funny that he met her at a fucking coffee shop.

"Sweetheart, would you like to tell Brady what you do for a living?" She swallows.

She looks between me and Brady, taking way too much time to answer me.

My patience is running out. I get up and walk to her. She cowers, backing up to the headboard.

She talks in a loud rush. "He paid me. Some guy paid me to keep him company." She points to Brady. "I thought he knew. The guy said it was a birthday gift."

"Who fucking paid you?"

"I don't know. I didn't ask him his name. I just knew it was a lot of money, and I took it."

She describes the guy, but it doesn't fit a description that I could fit with a name.

After the hooker gets finished talking, I let Brady know I intend to check on his whereabouts for the whole week.

When I start to leave the room, I turn to Brady. "If I find out different, I won't hesitate to call your uncle and let him know of the great punishment that you will be given. I promise you, it won't be something you can live through."

We leave Brady's house to discuss matters. Mark is close to finding out who is putting money into Hunter's account.

I tell Mark to check the GPS on Brady's SUV. If it's not Brady then some fucker we are dealing with seems to be not only screwing with Rose's family, but he chose the wrong men to mess with.

When I get back to Rose's apartment, I walk into the door, only to find Zane on the floor with a gash to the head. Yelling for Rose, I run to the bedroom, hoping to find her. She's not there. I storm into the bathroom, and there's no sign of her.

I yell out in frustration, "FUCK!"

I walk in long strides back to the living room and kick Zane in the leg.

"Get the fuck up!"

He moans. Putting his hand up to his forehead where the gash is, he wenches.

"What the hell happened here?" I bit out.

Zane pushes himself up and props himself up against the couch.

"Rose opened the door for some skinny fucker. He started yelling at her in the doorway about how her family had screwed him over. When he saw me, I started to get off the couch, but he got to me before I got up. He pulled out something sharp and hit me in the head," Zane says.

"Did you get a name or anything that could help us?"

Zane shakes his head.

I see Zane's cell lying on the floor, making me wonder if Rose has her phone. I pull out my phone and open the app I use to track her locations.

I see it—the red dot blinking on my screen—and she's not too far from us.

"Grab your shit. We have to go."

Mark rings me. "I've got him. I've got the name of the fucker who has been putting money into Rose's ex-boyfriend's account. I've done some digging into his background. Rose's dad bought his family's company because they were going bankrupt, and his dad committed suicide. Get this shit. You're not fucking going to believe who it is."

20

Rose

I'm blindfolded and lying in a fetal position in the trunk of a car that reeks of garbage. I've been trying to keep up with the movements, whether he's going right or left, but after a few turns, it seems like he is traveling in circles. I try to listen to the outside noises, but it seems to be all the same. Just cars honking and the hustle of the regular traffic in a city.

I try my best to unbind my wrists that are bounded behind my back, but it's no use. The twist tie doesn't budge.

There's no point in yelling because of the duct tape wrapped securely across my mouth.

I feel hopeless. I close my eyes and say a silent prayer that Blaze will be able to find me before it's too late.

Five minutes later, I hear the faint sounds of what could be motorcycles in the distance. They come to a loud roar. The rumble shakes the car. They must be right next to us. A biker screams out a profanity. I'm not sure if he's yelling in our direction or the direction of others.

I squint my eyes and do my best to look out of the tail-lights, but there must be black tape on the lights because I'm not able to make out even a hint of anything. There's only darkness.

The car comes to a halt, and I hear a sound resembling a car door being opened, and then screaming surrounds the vehicle.

Hope fills me. Could it be? Is that Blaze? The car shakes, and just as quickly as the vehicle stopped, it begins to move again.

The small amount of hope that I held is snuffed out.

Sometime later, I wake up. My head bobbin gives me the perfect view of my feet tied to a chair.

I must have drifted off to sleep. Raising my head to take in my surroundings, I let out a small shriek from the cramp in my neck.

The pulse in my ears pounds, causing a headache. The room is pitch-black, and my eyes won't focus. I blink several times, trying my best to make them come into focus.

I barely hear it, but there's a wrestling noise coming from my right side. Narrowing my eyes, I see what appears to be a black bag moving around on the floor.

What's in there? It has to be a significantly large animal. Fear flows through me. My eyes widen with horror. The bag is rolling on the floor. It could be a giant, wild beast that he put in here to eat me. I pull at the straps of my bonded hands. I have to get out of here. Then, a noise comes from the black bag—a muffle. Whatever it is, it's putting up one hell of a fight to get out of the bag.

After several moments of the beast struggling inside the bag, a head is freed. I gasp.

It's Lilly!

Relief fills me when I see my sister. I launch forward in the chair, hitting the concrete floor so hard that it breaks one of the wood legs.

Duct tape covers her mouth while her hands are bound in front of her. She's able to pull at the duct tape with her bounded hands. Once she rips it off, she breathes hard.

I look up at her, smiling on the inside. So happy to see my sister alive and well. I have no idea how long we will be alive, but I will try my best to fight out of this mess.

Lilly scoots over to where I'm lying on the floor, still tied to the chair. Taking her tied hands, she rips off the tape covering my mouth.

"Thank you," I whisper.

She looks around the dark room. "Look there." She points to the wall. "There's a covered window. We can escape through it."

I narrow my eyes, trying to see what she does. I see it now—the outline of what appears to be something covering a window.

"Quickly try to hit the zip tie on your shin," I tell Lilly.

"What? That's going to hurt," Lilly wines.

"Do it!"

Lilly hesitates but does what I tell her. She breaks the zip tie, making her hands accessible.

"What about my feet?" she asks.

"Take your shoes off and tie the laces together. You can use them to cut through the ties."

"Yes!" she says with excitement.

"Good, now help me get out of this chair."

Lilly uses her laces to cut through my ties. Once I'm untied and I have rubbed all the aches out, we walk to the wall. She runs her hands along the covering to feel if there is, somehow, a way we can remove it. We pry and pry till we pull it off the window. The light fills the room, giving a perfect view of a beautifully manicured lawn.

We smile at each other, the feeling of freedom in sight.

"Let's hurry before Trey comes back."

Lilly looks at me with concern, "Do you know him?"

"Yes, come on let's hurry."

"Get on my shoulders."

Lilly gets on my shoulders and pulls the window open then crawls out on the lawn.

Once Lilly is out, she reaches back for me to grab her hands.

I'm almost out of the hell where the son of a bitch threw us in, when, suddenly, the door swings open, and he stomps to me. Grabbing my legs, he pulls me in his direction while Lilly pulls me back in her direction, I kick and scream, but for a skinny ass, his grip doesn't loosen.

"Lilly, run. Go get Blaze." I do my best to push her,

but she won't let go. "Please just save yourself."

Trey has my body pulled halfway back into the room. I do my best to push Lilly off. I am telling her to run as far as she can. Finally, she listens to me as Trey pulls me back in. He throws me on the concrete floor. I lie there with pain running through my bones.

"Stupid bitch," he spits out at me. "Your sister might be gone to try and get help, but it'll be too late."

He kicks me.

"Don't get up," he shouts.

Moving back to the front door, he wrestles with a tripod. When he gets flustered with trying to put it up, he comes over and kicks me again but this time with more force.

He yells, "Fuck. Stay down."

He walks back over and finishes the tripod. He attaches his phone to it. Scanning the room, his eyes find a chair in the corner of the room. He goes to retrieve it, setting it in front of the camera.

Walking over to me, he leans down and grabs a hand-ful of my hair, pulling me up and walking me to sit in the chair.

I won't show weakness.

"What is the point of all this?" I ask with a steel in my voice.

"What is the point?" Trey says with a condescending voice. "Let me tell you." He shoves me into the chair and stands in my face. "I'm going to take away something your mother and father find very important. Just like your dad took away my father's business, causing him to kill himself."

"I have no idea what you are talking about. Just stop all this craziness and let me go!"

He laughs.

The slaps across my face come unexpectedly.

"Are you and Hunter in on this together?"

He laughs. "Hunter … Hunter couldn't pull fucking shit off. He's way too busy trying to get pussy off of the stupid bitches that work at that club."

Then it hits me. That was Bonnie, Hunter was fucking that day. The color of her hair with the blue streaks in it. I didn't put it together until now.

"Did Hunter kill Bonnie?" I bluntly ask.

Trey gives me a disappointed look. "Do you really think he could pull anything off like that? I'm so disappointed in you. Your not as smart as I had given you credit for."

"So it was you?"

"Bingo. We have a winner." He says as he claps his hands.

Asshole.

"Why did you kill Bonnie. Just because she was sleeping with Hunter?"

"Tiss Tiss, now do you really think I would give a shit if that whore was fucking him? She was fucking me too. When she found out about my plans because she was snooping around in my room that's when I knew it was time to take out the trash. So hanging her at the club was brilliant to get cops drawn there but then someone moved her body to her house."

"You won't get away with this Trey. Just let me go and stop all this."

***

Blaze

I'm still on the phone with Mark.

"I've got their location coordinates. I'm sending them to you. I'm leaving Rose's apartment and headed that way."

Calling the Anderson twins, I tell them where Rose's phone is.

Crew says, "We're outside the bar on 10th Street."

"They're moving along 9th Street. He drives an older sedan, white, with four doors."

Crew yells, "Fuck man, they're rounding the corner now. We're on it."

Crew starts his bike and hangs up.

Five minutes later, I'm in my car, headed in their direction, but traffic stops me. I punch the dash.

"Fucking aresholes!" I scream out the window to the other drivers.

Fucking New York traffic.

Twenty minutes later, I see the twins on the side of the street. Their bikes have flat tires.

"What the hell!" I yell out the window.

They run up and jump in the car.

"Fucking A, man. That skinny mother-fucker pulled a knife and slashed our tires. Then fucking said to stand back, or he would put a bullet in our foreheads."

"Fuck!"

That's it. I will kill him slowly by cutting him up limb by limb and throwing the parts in the river.

I'm on the path of the tracker when, all of a sudden, it goes blank.

NO!

We're out of the city, and Rose could be anywhere. I drive a few more miles, trying to decide where he would have taken her. There are country roads in all directions. I blow out air in frustration.

There's a figure running down a long dirt road.

Drew is sitting in the front seat and starts whistling. The fucker never stops thinking about pussy.

I shove him in the shoulder. Giving the figure a stern look, I realize who it is—Lilly.

"Shut the fuck up, Drew." I punch him.

Lilly is much too good for him.

She's still far from us. I drive up to meet her.

She's out of air. "Help … he has her." She barely musters up the words.

Drew jumps out, picks her up, and tells Crew to switch seats with him.

Drew sits in the back seat with Lilly, and once Crew climbs in, we move in the direction Lilly points to.

Five minutes later, we come to a crawl and stop in front of an old farmhouse.

Drew remarks, "I'll stay here with Lilly and ensure she's protected."

I give the fucker a look, and he smiles.

"Drew, put Lilly down and get your arse out," I command.

He sits her down while whispering in her ear.

We get out of the car as Mark pulls in behind us. Once he joins us, we look at the property.

"Lilly says he has her held up in the basement," I say.

"Let's go in there and just shoot him in the head," Crew remarks.

Drew replies back, "Fucker, we can't do that. He'll kill Rose before we get to him."

We finally agree on a plan. Everyone moves into place as I sneak around the house, looking in the windows as I go. I want to make sure we execute the plan in surprise.

I hear Trey's voice coming from a window that's located on the ground. I ease up, listening to what he says. Pulling out my cell, I text the men.

He's in the basement with Rose.

Mark replies.

I'm headed in the back door.

Crew replies.

We're standing on the front porch. It's unlocked; we're headed inside.

I hear Trey blaming Rose for his family issues. It pisses me off. I head back to the front of the house and enter through the front door. The men are waiting at what appears to be the door that enters the basement.

"Let me enter first," I whisper to them.

I pull my Glock out and draw it back. Everyone has

a smile on their face. Mark's smile is a little more twisted. He doesn't draw out a gun; instead, he pulls out a blade with jagged edges.

We take the steps one by one. There's no way in or out of the basement, except for the way we are entering.

The wood floor gives with each step we take. I'm on the last step, about to open the door, when it gives and collapses.

Fuck!

Not hesitating, I storm the room, gun drawn. Trey stands next to Rose with a gun to her head.

"Don't move, or I'll put a bullet in her skull," the fucker says.

Rose looks at me, and I can see tears starting to form.

I'm standing in the doorway, unsure if I want to take the chance of rushing him to free Rose. So, I do the only thing I can think of—negotiate.

"I'll put my gun down if you move yours away from Rose. Point it at me—that's fine—but move it away from Rose."

"You just put your gun down and shut the fuck up."

I'm trying to be patient, but this little fucker is pissing me off.

Trey laughs, and for a split second, he moves the gun away from Rose. Then, a loud bang occurs, and a sharp object grazes my ear, making its way into Trey's forehead.

Epilogue

Two Years Later

Rose

It's been two years since the crazy incident happened. Feeling blood splatter onto my face was not the finest moment I'd ever had, but the embrace of large arms wrapping around me afterward made it worth it. Crew took the shot that cost Trey his life. Blaze's ear was skinned a bit, but the bullet didn't cause any real damage, just a little scratch.

Trey's body was never found. I don't think anyone will miss him. He had no family left. His mother left his father when he was only a toddler, and because of their selfish ways, they drove everyone else away when they were rich.

My father's customers came back after Trey was killed. Trey was poaching his customers and promising them all kinds of rewards for a low price. I think he got in over his head because he couldn't fulfill their needs.

I finally finished my law degree. A lawyer position at Ross and Archer became open, and I was accepted for the job. I still work at Red, just less. I enjoy the atmosphere of the club, and I get to spend more time with Blaze. Occasionally, I see Mr. Wallace and his brother at Red, but they don't tend to flirt any longer, and a big reason is Blaze having a heated word with them.

We land at Kitty Hawk and plan to spend the week with my family. We're meeting Lilly and her high school sweetheart at the center, where we have decided to host an anniversary party for my parents.

Blaze pulls the rental car up to the center, and Lilly stands at the doorway, waiting on us. I get out of the car and run to hug her.

"Hey!" I scream out, giving her a bear hug.

Lilly barely hugs me back. I give her a look of disappointment.

Blaze walks up and embraces Lilly. She finally smiles.

"Let's go inside and see how it looks. I haven't been here since we had Nana's birthday party. That was like, what, fifteen years ago?" I smile at Lilly.

Lilly's smile doesn't reach the corners of her mouth.

"Do you want to talk about it?" I ask.

Her mood must be about her boyfriend. I don't see him in sight. I can't imagine why she would be in such a sour mood.

Lilly shakes her head. I drop the subject. We run through the center, pointing out how we can decorate. Once we finish, we load up in our vehicles and head to our parents' house.

Once we arrive at my parents'. Mom runs to us, giving hugs and kisses to me and Lilly, but when she sees Blaze, she squeals with excitement.

"Oh, Blaze." Mom embraces Blaze harder. "It's always so good to see you."

I roll my eyes at her tone of voice. The way she

overacts around him is sickening. She might as well be president of his fan club.

The bond my family has with Blaze has made life easy. It's hard when your family disapproves of your boyfriend. It's also gross how my mother drools over my man.

"Come in, come in. You're staying with us. We have two rooms set up. Blaze, you will be in the blue room, and the girls will be in the yellow room."

I can't help but laugh at the look on Blaze's face. The look of horror that he will have to do without sex for a week.

Blaze leans into my ear. "I'm coming to get you when your parents go to bed. I'm not going a week without that sweet pussy."

I shove him in the ribs.

He chuckles.

The next few days go smoothly. We have all the decorations in place and all the food ordered. Now, we sit back and enjoy the show.

When I say show, I mean, *show*. My family is a circus. My mother's brother, who's in his forties, is a man who has drama issues. I can't remember one family gathering where he's not been a hot, drunken mess, spilling out his sex escapades and trying to hit on my grandmother, which is my dad's mom. It has been so bad in the past that my grandmother moved and wouldn't give anyone her address for over a year. My father's family thinks they are better than anyone, but when my dad's sister fell out of the coat closet, naked with the server's dick in her mouth, it brought her high and mighty self down a bit. Who can blame her? The man had a huge cock, but her husband wasn't happy about it. Nevertheless, this is my fucked up family, and I love them.

We're seated at the table across from my parents, who are so happy that we planned this party for them. Blaze has disappeared for a few minutes, and Lilly won't stop playing with her cake.

"Lilly, do you want to talk about it?" I ask her for the tenth time.

She shakes her head and goes back to playing with her cake.

Someone clears their throat and clanks their silverware against a glass. I look around the room until I spot him. Blaze is walking in the middle of the room to me.

He clanks his glass again getting everyone's attention.

He clears his throat and starts to make a toast.

I roll my eyes. *Figures.*

I glance over at my mom. I know she has to be in hog heaven.

"The reason why we are here today is to celebrate the relationship of Mr. and Mrs. Sterling. Their marriage is what every couple should strive for."

Blaze comes and stands behind his chair.

He goes on bended knee. "Rose, will you marry me?"

He holds up a diamond ring that sparkles.

"Yes!" I scream out. I jump up and tackle him, causing us to fall over. Grabbing his face, I pull his lips to meet mine, kissing him passionately.

The End